# GREATNESS PASSED ON

MICHAEL GOLDSMITH

ISBN: 978-1-5356-1564-8

*Dedication*

I would like to dedicate this book to Jim Erickson. He coached for years at Carton High School.
He was the coach that his players loved. Thank you Coach for teaching me that hard work produces true lasting results.

I want to thank Ruby the young lady who painted the cover.
Elizabeth Walton who did my editing.
Thank You.
If a person looks in the Back of Eli Greatness Begins they will See all the sponcers who believed in the work God the Father had given me to do.
Thank you to all of them.
And most important.
My family. Without them putting up with Dad and Gramps none of this would have happened.

# Contents

# Herman

ELI WALKED INTO THE KITCHEN. Tears had been flowing from the eyes of all the members of his family because of the loss of Jamaal. On Friday, they had watched Herman pitch in the Little League World Series. On Tuesday of the following week, they were at a funeral for the great Jamaal Johnson. He had gone back into the ghetto to try to reach his friends for Christ.

Eli took his beautiful bride of seventeen years into his arms and cried on her shoulder. "Hun, I have poured myself into helping these kids. I gave ten years of my life to get Jamaal to where he could be a great player and put himself into a situation where he could speak into young people's lives." He stepped back, grabbed a cloth rag off the sink, and threw it across the kitchen. "I have had it. We are done. We are leaving this jungle and going to find a place where we can raise our kids in peace. I will not put my kids at risk with these thugs here anymore."

Peter looked over at the Father. "Did you put this on Eli's heart, or is he just totally fed up with the whole situation?"

The Father smiled. "Peter, I want to get Herman and his little sister into a location that is going to be a place of peace for their growing-up years. I am going to use Herman in ways that are totally different from his dad, but his ministry is going to be one of power and grace. It is going to start when he plays ball in high school, and then it will follow him into a successful career."

Peter looked at the Father as he asked, "Another great baseball career I presume?"

The Father again smiled. "Pete, stay tuned. This one is going to be full of something special."

Over the next few weeks Eli would spend time looking to northern Minnesota. The Holy Spirit would keep leading him to one small town. He would spend time with Dave Beck, realtor extraordinaire to find the perfect place to raise his kids. He walked into the kitchen, walked up behind Jill, put his harms around her and she turned. "Sweetheart I have some news for you. We are moving back to Minnesota."

Jill looked lovingly into Eli's eyes. "Babes, do we want to go back to Roseau?"

Eli chuckled. "No, that's not where I feel like we should go. I was looking at a map of Northern Minnesota.

Look here. This little dot. Carlton, Minnesota. That's where we are going. I spoke with my realtor, Dave Beck, and he pointed out a nice country estate." With that, he showed Jill a picture of a white house on a hill, surrounded by pines trees, and overlooking a beautiful little pond.

Jill smiled as she said, "When can we fly to Minnesota and see it?"

Eli got a grin on his face. "Babes, you will see your new home in a few days. We move in five days. This house goes on the market next week. We will already be in Minnesota."

Jill looked at Eli. She had a question that she had to ask. "Hun, since when do you make decisions of this level without my input?"

The look on Eli's face said only one thing, "Father please help me!" "Hun, I am sorry, things were happening so quickly, I just wanted to get out of here."

Jill smiled and walked over to Eli. She put her arms around his neck. "Babes, I learned a long time ago that you know the Father's heart. The love you have shown all of us is so amazing. I would have appreciated being involved, but I do know that when God our Father is in the middle of something, it works. Let's go to Minnesota."

Pete looked over at the Father. "Is life going to be a cake walk for Herman now?" he asked.

The Father looked back. "No, Pete, what Eli is going to find out is that many of the same problems exist in a small town that do in a big town. The difference is that Herman is about to find out what a big fish in a small pond really means. The impact Herman Mcbrien is going to have at Carlton High School is going to be totally awesome. People's lives are going to be changed because I am bringing him into this small community. You had better get Thumbnail ready. Herman is going to have every young lady in Carlton drooling over him. However, Herman is going to be one 'set apart' for my glory. For the next few years, this little town of Carlton is going to be at the center of everything I am going to do to touch the hearts of people all over the world."

Peter looked at the Father of all mankind and asked, "Father how are you going to use such a little hamlet to touch the world with your greatness?"

The Father looked at his son Jesus the Christ, who was sitting on the throne to his right and smiling because he knew what was coming, and replied, "Pete, this ride Herman is about to start is going to have people talking all over the country. The stories will be astounding for this little school. What the students in this school are about to experience will change their lives forever. You see, Peter, when I take one person and drop them into a situation that I have created especially for them, the results are amazing. The brains and athletic ability I have built into this kid are going to astonish people. When I said he will touch millions, I meant it.

Through him, we will see kids come to me that were totally lost. My Spirit in a person gives that person the ability to do exactly what I created them to do. Pete, hold on, this is going to be a wild ride."

The next morning ushered in a hot July day. Eli, Jill, and Herman were packing up the house, and the movers were loading the truck. Herman was feeling down; leaving his buddies in California was not something he wanted to do. The thought of moving to a town that was so small if you blinked you might miss it, did not really excite him. He sat behind his parents for many hours with a grumpy look on his face.

The family drove across the country in their new motorhome. At this point in his life, Herman had only known California. They got off the freeway at the Carlton exit and headed for the little town of Carlton, Minnesota.

"Dad, can we just drive by the school? I have to see it." Herman asked.

With a smile on his face, Eli answered, "Yup! and they turned towards the school. As they drove by the school Herman smiled and said. "Mom, Dad this is a pretty small school. I hope that the kids are not too 'cliquey."

"Dad just think how much better Jamaal's life would have been if he had grown up in a place like this, rather than L.A." Herman thought out loud.

"Son, in a town like this, it is easier to keep kids out of big trouble. Yet, if a kid wants trouble, he will find it. The one thing you won't find here are gangs. You won't find warfare in the streets. But trouble? It's always there if a kid wants it." Eli responded.

Herman got a quizzical look on his face. "But Dad, why would a kid want to find trouble?"

"Son, kids whose families are not Christ-centered may have no moral compass to guide them. Kids are looking to fill that hole in their heart that is God-sized. They have to fill it with something. They will either fill it with Christ or they will fill it with whatever Satan has in store for them. All you have to do is look at Jamaal's life. His family was the gang. It ended up costing that little redheaded boy his life on this earth. Yet it was the loss of that boy's life that brought Jamaal to his knees. What loss is worth the gain? That's God's call, not mine."

Having driven around the school, Eli had turned towards the country where their new estate was located. The farm had been in one family for close to a hundred years. He drove the eight miles from Carlton to the riverside road that the little farm was on. As he drove around the little pond that the house overlooked, he pulled the motorhome over. He, Jill, and Herman got out of the vehicle, and they all stood and looked at the beautiful place where they would be living. "Pretty view, if I do say so myself."

Jill got that sly grin on her face. "What do you mean, yourself? What did you have to do with building that?"

"Shall we go up the driveway and look at our new home? After all, I did buy it." Eli said, not wanting to address the question Jill had asked.

They went around the next bend in the road and looked up their driveway for the first time. It was a somewhat narrow hill, heavily forested on both sides of the driveway. Eli looked over at Jill and said, "This hill will be paved in two weeks."

As they reached the top of the hill, the look on Jill's face changed from one of doubt to one of surprise and awe. "Eli, this is so very beautiful. But so many trees. How can we possibly build a new horse barn with no pasture land?"

"Relax, hun," Eli said. "The previous owners told me about a company that will clear cut it and pay us for the lumber. I will also have them remove the stumps. We will have horses on this land by next year." As they pulled up next to the house. Eli wanted to do something as soon as they got out of the car. "I think we need to pray before we start our new adventure in this place. God our Father through His Son Jesus by His Holy Spirit has led us here. Let's pray. Father, you have had many children raised on this farm. I can feel the peace was here for the Goldsmith family for generations.

I pray first that you will continue to bless the families that have grown here. I pray that you will grant success to each of the family members as they go about their lives from this point on. Father, we now come to you as the newest family that you are going to be raising a family on this little piece of heaven. As my son and daughter grow here I pray that you will touch their lives with the same peace you have granted everyone who has lived here in the past. I pray, Father, that you will grant me the wisdom to lead my family in your ways and with a heart for your Son the Christ that will never be broken.

I pray for the friendships that Herman and little Sharon develop over the years. I pray that you will teach them things on this land that will continue with them forever. In Jesus Name, Amen."

With that, 15-year-old Herman got out of the motorhome. He walked around the house. "Dad, Mom, no car noise. All I hear are crickets." he said.

The 18-month-old Sharon started to run across the soft grass on the lawn. Her giggles rang to the housetop. She stood at the edge of the lawn, looking over the expanse of lawn that used to be a hayfield. Her golden hair blew in the wind and her blue eyes sparkled in the sunlight.

"Dad, it snows here, right?" Eli asked.

"Yes, Son, it snows here. Why do you ask?"

Herman got a worried look on his face. "That means there will be a lot of snow on this driveway, right?" he answered.

"Herman, come with me." his dad said. They walked over to the garage. Eli pointed to a snow shovel leaning up against the side of the garage. "See that, Son?" he asked Herman.

"Ahhh, Dad, what do you have in mind?" Herman was thinking his dad was going to have him shovel a quarter-mile driveway with a snow shovel. His eyes started to get big with fear.

Eli got one of those sly grins on his face he used to get when he was young and about to pull a huge prank on one of his sisters. "Herman just think how shoveling the length of the driveway could strengthen your pitching arm!"

Herman's eyes widened as Eli told him to pick up the shovel and come with him. They walked around to the back side of the garage. Herman turned the corner of the garage and saw a huge snow blower attachment fixed to the tractor sitting behind it.

"Herman, that is what you're going to use to clean the driveway. I will teach you how to run it. This farm will become a place of refuge for you and your sister in years to come. God is going to bless this place. You will have so many great memories of this place. Let's start to have some fun with it." Eli said.

When Herman saw the blower, he got a big smile on his face. He relaxed and thought of how exciting it would be run that blower after a huge Minnesota snowstorm. He could hardly wait for the snow to fly so he could start to have some fun.

Eli walked over to Herman. "Son, I think it's time we get the rest of the household stuff put in the house for your mother. We both grew up in the country, and she knows how much work it's going to be. We have to do all that we can to make things as easy as possible for her." Eli said with a great deal of enthusiasm.

The next eight hours were spent helping to unload two semi-truck loads of furniture. After a full day's work, they headed into Carlton to have dinner at the Street Car Diner, and then they headed back to the farm where they would be sleeping in the motorhome for a few nights until they got the house set up just the way Jill wanted it.

Jill did everything she could to help the men with the unloading projects they needed to accomplish, but her main job was keeping a close eye on sweet little Sharon.

"Pete, see the little girl I created? Look how that beautiful blonde hair shines in the sunlight. Notice the sparkle in those blue eyes I have given her. She is going to be a blessing to the young man I have started to prepare for her." Just then, Hanna came running up with the little redhaired boy.

"Father, is my sister Sharon going to be a great servant of yours? Is she going to be used to draw lots of people into your kingdom?" Hanna asked with pure joy in her heart.

The Father smiled and simply nodded. Joy filled Hanna's heart as she realized just how exciting it would be when Sharon reached heaven, so she could share the joy of all her years and hard work and adventures with Hanna.

Eli stood on the edge of the lawn looking at the driveway that went between the house and the pump house. He looked at the woods that used to be a pasture that fed the livestock the family used to have there. He knew that the Berthumes could have that logged in one winter. He had negotiated with them for all the stumps to be removed and leveled so livestock could graze there again. In his mind he saw two horses grazing in the pasture land – one a tall quarter horse named Blaze and the other a Shetland pony named Rideaway.

Jill walked up behind Eli. She put her arms around his waist. He turned his head and smiled. "What are you thinking, hun?" she asked.

Eli smiled with a gentle smile as the occasion demanded. "I saw two horses grazing in the pasture land. A quarter horse named Blaze and a Shetland pony named Rideaway for Sharon. I really think having horses is going to do a great things for the kids. It will give them some responsibility as well as build a real love for animals." he said.

Jill smiled, kissed him on the cheek, and said. “Hun, all those years in the city did not take the country boy out of you. Granted you were raised in a small town, but you are all country.”

Eli smiled knowing just how much Jill loved and respected him. They looked at their two children: Herman, who they knew was destined for something great, and Sharon, who was a bundle of love that somehow would change the world for better.

They looked at the ten acres of lawn. Eli shook his head. “How are we going to care for all of that?” he said. Then the thought hit his brain like a lightning bolt. “You know, Sweetheart, with the money we have we could hire someone to mow all of this for us, or we could put the kids to work. Personally, I think putting the kids to work is a much better idea. During the summer, we are looking at three days a week for that lawn to be mowed. We could pay the kids, well, pretty much Herman for next few years anyway, to keep the lawn in shape. Then when Sharon gets old enough we can put her to work as well.”

Just then Herman came jumping off the front porch onto the lawn. He landed on his feet after jumping off the cement steps. Eli turned to him and asked one little question. “Having fun?”

“Dad, I love this place! It’s gonna be so much fun! I saw you looking at the field. What are you thinking about, Dad?” Herman asked.

Eli got an impish grin on his face when he knew he was going to do something fun. "Herm, I was just thinking of how to keep this huge lawn mowed now that it belongs to us."

"How? Who are you going to hire to do it?" Herm asked.

"We are not going to hire anyone, Son. You are going to do it. I just ordered a new push mower. That should keep you busy every day this summer." was the sly answer that Eli gave Herm.

"Dad, you expect me to mow that whole thing by hand?" Herm answered with a note of fear in his voice.

Eli chuckled a bit as he answered, "Naaa! I just ordered that for the trimming around the trees. I also ordered a new John Deere lawn tractor with a mower for you to use. You should be able to get it mowed in about three days. You will receive some compensation for your work." At that point, one could almost see the dollar signs going through Herman's head as he asked. "How much am I going to make?"

Eli, in a matter of fact way said, "$25."

"Dad, that's not much for all of the hours it will take to get this done." Herm responded.

"Herman, my boy, I think that is a fair wage. Everything else in your life is covered." With that, Eli turned and walked back in the house. Just before he opened the door, he turned and said. "Oh, yeah! The tractor gets delivered tomorrow. I will give you a quick lesson, and off you'll go." With a slight grin, he turned and went into the house.

That night Herman went to bed early. He was totally exhausted. He went to sleep quickly. Then at about 4:00 a.m., he heard the sweet song of a bird singing just outside his window. He got up quietly and snuck over to the window to see a robin sitting on the telephone wire attached to his house singing for its mate. Smiling, he turned and went downstairs and walked out onto the back porch, looking off to the east. He stood there looking out into the darkness. The eastern sky started to turn a light orange. It continued getting brighter and brighter. The sun started to peek over the horizon. The day was beginning.

Just then he heard his dad Eli come through the back door. "Morning, Son." Eli said.

"Morning, Dad." Herman responded. "Dad, this place is beautiful, I can almost feel all the people who have lived here before us. I was thinking that I really don't need to be paid for mowing the lawn. How about I take care of the lawn? When I need a few bucks for something I will just ask for it. I am your son, not an employee. I really need to do things just as a part of this family. Dad, I love you and Mom. God spoke to me while I was lying in bed this morning. Jesus did not ask his Father for money for what he did for us. Mowing the lawn is something I can do to help the family."

Eli smiled, put his hand on his son's shoulder. "I love you too, Son, and it's time to go to work."

# A New Way of Life

OVER THE NEXT FEW WEEKS, the farm was a very busy place. Eli contacted the logging company and they started working on turning the forest back into pasture land. The mowers were delivered so Herman could keep the lawn looking nice. Builders came in to rebuild the barn, and Eli started putting new fence posts in to prepare for the horses in that he planned to buy.

Tuesday of their first week in their new home, the Kinkaid family stopped by to meet their new neighbors. They had three children, two boys and a young girl about Sharon's age. The two boys were active in 4H and also involved in the football program at Carlton. They just happened to have a football in their car. Jake, the oldest of the boys, tossed one to Herman. Herman caught it and looked at the ball. Herman then threw a short pass to Jake, who ran a quick route, and hit him right in the hands. Jake got a look on his face that said, "this kid looks good."

"Have you ever thought of playing football?" Jake asked. "In baseball, if you have a great pitcher, like your dad, he can control games. I remember hearing an interview with

Sam Boursa who said that sometimes it got really boring playing the outfield when your dad was pitching. No one could hit him. In football, you can have a great quarterback, but without the supporting players, he goes nowhere. At the same time, without a great quarterback, the team suffers a lot. Practice starts August 21. Can you make it?"

Herman looked at his dad. Eli smiled as he said, "You wanna play football, go for it. They will probably recruit you for basketball as well. It will keep you in shape to play baseball in the spring."

Herman looked over at Jake and said, "Set, hut!"

Pete looked over at the Father. "Looks like you have got another winner here, Father."

The Father of all mankind smiled, and heaven lit up. "Remember I told you there would never be a better pitcher than Eli? It's the same with Herman. Only he is going to be the best quarterback ever to step on a football field. Remember this: I create people to accomplish great things. I create people to bring honor to whatever field I put them in. As people work in their fields of expertise and they give the glory to me, I give glory back to them. Herman has a quick mind. He will be able to find the open receiver. He will also be able to change the play at the line of scrimmage. This is going to be fun!"

Eli looked over at his son throwing the football to his buddies. He could not help but let his mind go back to that day when the doctor told him he had to have his hips fixed and the fear that had gone through him. He remembered that long-ago day in January when his mom woke him up so very early to go work out. He remembered his first runner's high. He remembered the first time he heard "Secret Ambition" and how it became his theme song when he was on the mound. He could not help but wonder what would drive Herman.

The Father was smiling. He turned to His Son Jesus and said, "I have created a young man with a heart towards me that will not be stopped. As kids are drawn to Herman, they will be drawn to me. I will put it on his heart to work with kids of every denomination: Catholics, Lutherans, Baptists, Assembly of God. You name it, he will work with them. But the truly exciting stuff will come after he finishes as a pro.

Jesus smiled and walked over to the Father. The little redheaded boy and Hanna came running up to Jesus. Jesus touched them both and smiled. Hanna looked at Herman down on earth. "Father how great a football player will he be?"

Jesus smiled and looked at the Father. Jesus said, "You know what the Father tells Peter when he asks those kinds of questions? He tells him to just stay tuned. Little Hanna, stay tuned. You are in for a fun ride seeing what is going to happen with him."

Eli prayed right then for his son that no surgery like he had experienced would ever be needed by Herman. He also prayed that the platform that Herman would be given would be able to touch kids all over the world with the love and faithfulness of the Christ.

The Father looked at Peter and said, "Herman is going to have something that Eli did not. He is going to have the love and support of a great father. My Son Jesus paid a great price so that fathers would be able to lead their sons and daughters to me. Every dad has the choice to be a great dad or not. Eli has chosen to be a great dad. The success of his kids will be a testament to his greatness and mine.

## The Start of Something Big in the Fall

It was now the first day of football practice. The dreaded two-a-days. Herman walked into the locker room for the first time, not knowing what to expect. Coach Erickson walked up to him and put his right hand on Herman's left shoulder.

"Son, I hear you've got an arm that won't quit. You can throw a football 60 yards in the air as a freshman. Now, in baseball a pitcher has one job, throw a controlled ball. In football, the quarterback must know what every man on his team must do on every play."

Herm looked at his coach and asked one short question: "When can I see the playbook?"

Coach Erickson gave a little chuckle. "Right now." He handed the playbook to Herman who opened it, looked at the Xs and Os, and got a look on his face that said "HELP!"

Coach Erickson chuckled a bit. "Son, this is a 29-counter reverse." The blank look on Herman's face was telling. "Herman this is a misdirection play. It's like when you throw a sinker that looks like it is going to cross the plate and just before it gets there it drops like a rock. You see, what your running back will start to do is drive to the 1-hole, which is on the left side. The line then starts to drive like they are going to go to that hole. Everyone takes the first step to the left, then they counter to the right, with the running back making a drive to the right. But if you look over here to the right, you see the wide receiver starts to the left. By this time, the whole defense is moving to the right. The running back hands the ball off to the wide receiver, who should have a clear shot to the end zone." Coach Erickson looked at his very green quarterback. "All you have to do is know where every player on your team is at every second of the game. Think you can do that?"

"Not only can I do that, I will be the best quarterback ever to come out of Carlton High School!" Herman responded.

Coach Erickson chuckled to himself as he replied, "Son, it's time to see what you're made of. I want you dressed in your shorts, t-shirt, and shoulder pads in twenty minutes and on the practice field with the rest of the team. Then we'll see what you can do."

Twenty minutes later, Herman jogged onto the football field. He looked around and saw the rest of the team. There seemed to be a dread, yet excitement amongst the whole team. One of the seniors, Dennis Wolf, walked up to Herm and said bluntly, "I hope you worked out over the summer. If not, the next two weeks will be brutal." He turned and walked away.

Herman's face started to turn white. "*What have I gotten myself into?*" he thought. Coach Erickson came running out. "Gentlemen remember this: the next two weeks of training will be tough. You're not training for the first quarter of a game. You're not training for the for the fourth quarter. You're training for the last two minutes of a tie game. You're training for the time you have nothing left in you physically, and you have to dig deep to find that last ounce of strength to push the ball into the end zone or keep our opponent out of our end zone." With that, he turned to his assistant coach, Jim Kuklis, nodded, and watched them go to work.

The next two weeks were indeed brutal for Herman. He felt muscles he had never known he had. Yet, at the end of the two weeks of two-a-days, he felt a sense of accomplishment he never known before.

Arriving at the front door of Carlton High School on his first day of school, the very first thing he noticed was the statue of the Bulldog in front of the school. As he walked on campus for the first time, he could tell right away it was a school full of spirit. What he was not expecting was the reaction of the rest of the students to the boy from California.

Walking down the hall, he immediately noticed a bully picking on a 7th-grade kid. He walked up to the bully and said with a great deal of authority for a 9th-grader, "If I were you, I would not pick on kids younger than you are."

"Listen, Preppy, if I were you I would mind my own business." The bully said in a threatening tone.

Herman shook his head. The bully was much bigger than Herman, but his dad had always taught him to meet force with force. He went toe to toe with the bully and said, "Listen, I don't know who you are, and I really don't care. If you don't leave the younger kids alone, I may just have to break your arm." he said with total self-assurance.

The bully grabbed Herman by the neck. Herman quickly remembered everything his "Aunt" Corrine had taught him back in California. He had the brute's arm around behind him and his own arm around the bully's neck in a split second. He got close to the bully's ear and said very clearly. "If you ever, I mean ever, touch any of the students in this school again, your arm that I have now behind your back will be in a cast for at least six weeks. Is that understood?" Herman said.

"Yes, Sir!" The bully stammered. "May I ask what your name is?"

"I am Herman Mcbrien."

"You're the son of Eli Mcbrien?"

"The same."

After a short pause, the bully finally said, "Herman, welcome to Carlton. You can count on me, there will no longer be bullies in this school."

As Herman walked down the halls the rest of the day he was treated like a conquering hero. It seemed that everyone was looking up to him, and he had not even stepped on the football field yet. As he walked around the school everyone was very friendly. But then he noticed that there were some kids who no one talked to or included at all; it was like they were not even noticed.

Peter looked over at the Father. "Is Herman going to realize that there is another type of bullying going on here? Is it the bullying of ignoring that is coming into play? It's the bullying of a student not being thought good enough to be included?"

The Father looked over at Peter and said. "Watch and learn, Pete. Watch and learn."

Herman spotted one such person. She was a cute freshman named Allison. "HI, there." Herman said.

"Hello." Alli replied.

"May I ask why you are here all alone? It seems like everyone is busy with their friends and having a good time between classes." Herman asked.

Alli got a look of anger and despair on her face as she replied, "It seems if one does not wear the right clothes or have the right parents, that one is just not included in the "in" group. Even in a small school like this there are cliques. If you're a jock or a cheer leader or have money, then you're accepted. If not, then oh well." Alli shrugged her shoulders as if she wanted this to not matter so much.

"Hmmm, another form of bullying that has to be put to an end. Alli, what lunch do you have today?" Herman asked.

"I am on the third lunch."

"Why don't we have lunch together?"

Alli got a questioning look on her face. "Why would you have lunch with me?" she asked.

"Just have lunch with me. You will see what I am going to do to stop this bullying. It may take a while, but we will end it."

Peter looked over at the Father. "What do you have in mind here, Father? Seems to me that there is something cooking."

With a chuckle, the Father responded, "Pete, if I told you everything, then where would the surprise be? Let's just say some bullies are about to get a taste of their own medicine."

The third lunch bell rang. Herman walked down the ramp into the cafeteria and spotted Alli sitting by herself at a long lunch table. The "in" group was sitting at another table. Herman got his lunch and walked over to the table Alli was sitting at and sat across from her. As they started eating and talking, the neighboring group started to make their way over to the table. Alli looked at Herman and smiled. Herman held his hand up and winked. Herman turned and looked at the table where the "in" group had just been sitting, and he smiled to himself.

"C'mon, Alli. Let's find a table where the repugnant smell of self-importance is not quite so strong." With that, they both got up from the table and moved to the empty table where the "in" crowd had been just moments ago.

The "in"group sat at their new table with their jaws hanging open. They had all just been hit between the eyes with a truth bullet for the first time in their lives, and they were not quite sure how to handle it. One young lady named Janet got up from the table and walked over to the table Alli and Herman were sitting.

"I am so sorry for what I have been doing. I realized it wasn't very kind, but I wanted to be part of the group. I am going to work to change things around here." Janet said.

"Pete, you see, all it takes one person to change the mindset of hundreds. Herman just got a taste of what that one person looks like in himself. He also realized the feeling of accomplishment that I give a person when they surrender to me and I use them to make huge changes." the Father said.

That night was the first freshman football game of the year. Carlton played Moose Lake. The score was very lopsided as Carlton scored five unanswered touchdowns. Herman threw for three of those touchdowns and ran for one more. Coach Erickson took note of each touchdown and every pass completion.

After the game he walked up to Herman and said, "Herman, you are dressing for the varsity game. I have no backup quarterback, and you know the offense. If I need you, I want you dressed so I can use you."

Friday morning, the day of the first varsity game came. Eli grabbed his game jersey, put it on, and headed to school. That afternoon at the pep rally, the student body was in full cheer. The team was introduced. The Coach went through each class from seniors down to sophomores. Then, to the surprise of everyone, he announced "and a freshman, Herman Mcbrien." The crowd went wild as Herman walked out to the center of the gym. Alli smiled broadly as her new friend was introduced to the school.

At dinner that night Eli looked across the table at his son. "Herm, I hear you are shaking things up at Carlton. Is there anything I need to be aware of?"

Herman got a broad smile as he said. "Dad, what have you heard?"

"Herman, I got two phone calls from the office in the last week. One to tell me you just about broke another students arm, and another to tell me a group of students came to sit with you and a young lady and you made a snide remark and got up and left the table with the young lady. What do you have to say about those things?" his dad asked with a concerned voice.

Herman smiled and asked, "What else did they say about what happened?" knowing the way his dad was stating the facts did not look very good.

Thumbnail asked, "Father, may I come into your presence?"

The Father smiled, "Of course, my littlest angel. What would you like?"

"Will you use me with Herman as you used me with Eli?" Thumbnail asked humbly.

"Stand by," was the Father's answer.

Eli had a look of question on his face. "What do you mean?"

"Did they tell you the person whose arm I almost broke was bullying a younger student?" Herman asked his dad.

"Or did they tell you that the young lady I was sitting with a lunch was all alone, having had the backs of every person from the "in" crowd turned on her?"

Eli walked over to his son and put his arm around his shoulders. "Nope, they left those details out. Looks to me like you took care of some bullies. I am proud of you son."

That night in the varsity game against Moose Lake, Carlton was not having a great game. They were down 24-0 at the half. The coach looked to John Johnson his senior quarterback. "I think it's time to make a change. I am going to sit you, John, for your own protection. Their defense has been all over you. Mcbrien, you're in the second half."

"Yes, sir!" Herman said. Carlton received the ball first in the second half.

Coach Erickson pulled Herman over. "I want a 29 fly. Look for Wolf streaking down the left sideline. You should be able to hit him flat out into the end zone. Roll to your left for the best vision. Their rushers come right up the middle."

Herman ran out to the huddle and looked at his teammates. "29 fly, on set. Wolf, I am looking for you to be open down the left sideline. Let's make it happen!"

The team broke the huddle. Herman went under and called out the signals. The ball was snapped. Herman rolled to his left. He spotted Wolf down the sidelines and threw a perfect pass. It landed softly right into Wolf's hands who then took it into the end zone for a touchdown.

The rest of the game was not quite as pretty. The defensive coach of the Lakers was able to figure out the new alignments against the Bulldogs quite easily as Herman was not as familiar with the offense that was needed for this game.

In the locker room after the game the guys were feeling down, to say the least. They had just lost the game 56 to 7. The Bulldogs were devastated. They had not lost a game by such a lopsided score ever. Coach Erickson walked into the locker room with a smile on his face. "Gentlemen, congrats to you. You have done something no other Bulldog team has ever accomplished. You gave up 56 points." He turned and walked out.

Practice the next Monday was nothing short of brutal. Coach had them running and running the whole practice. After practice Coach Erickson pulled the defense aside. "You will never let another team into my end zone again, will you?"

"No Sir!" the team yelled in unison.

The Father looked over at Peter, then to his Son sitting on his right as he said," You're about to see a steel wall go up. You're about to understand what an immovable object is all about. This coach is about to teach one of my most basic truths. You don't compromise on that which is right. That's what the steel wall is all about."

The rest of the week's practices went as usual. Herman worked on the offensive plays as the back-up quarterback. He ran the back-up offense against the starting defense. Every play they tried to run was stuffed. He knew Cromwell was in big trouble come Friday night.

Friday came quickly. As the team was in the locker room suiting up, Herman was led to go over and talk to the senior quarterback, John Johnson. "John, I feel like I am supposed to pray for you." Herman said.

"I don't need your prayer mumbo jumbo. I am fine all by myself." Johnson said with total pride.

Peter looked at the Father and said, "Father, are you going to use this as a teaching situation for John?"

The Father smiled and said, "Stay tuned, Peter. Stay tuned."

The first quarter of the game was the only one that John would play in. He threw two interceptions and fumbled the ball once. At the start of the second quarter, Coach Erickson put his right hand on John's shoulder and said, "John, you're done tonight. Have a seat."

As Herman walked by John, he said quietly, "You should have let me pray for you." Herman walked up to Coach Erickson. The coach looked at him with a smile

"29 fly. Look for Wolf again."

"Gotcha, Coach!" was Herman's reply. He trotted to the huddle, looked at his players, and said, "29 fly. Coming your way Denny. On one. Let's make this work. Break!"

The team broke the huddle. Herman called out the signals. The ball was snapped. Herman rolled to the left and spotted Denny Wolf flying down the sideline. He threw a perfect 50-yard strike. Touchdown! Carlton went on to defeat Cromwell 24-0, for the first of many shutouts that year.

After the game the teammates walked into the locker room. John walked up to Herman and asked if he could talk to him. "Sure!" was Herman's happy reply.

The Father looked at Gabe. "It's time to bring Thumbnail in. Herman is going to be a huge influence on Carlton High School. His influence starts now."

Gabe moved over to the angels' quarters. "Thumbnail! Front and center!" he yelled.

Thumbnail came flying out of the quarters. "Do I get to go to work again?" he asked excitedly.

The Father looked at Thumbnail and smiled. "You sure do, my little one. You sure do."

John looked intently at Herman. "Look, you're a freshman. You have never played this game before. You have the ability to throw the ball and hit a dime at 50 yards. I have never seen a freshman throw a ball like that. Where does all that talent come from?"

Herman looked at him and said, "It's a gift from God. We are all given gifts. It's a matter of how hard we are willing to work with the gifts we have been given. It doesn't matter if it's acting, being able to fix cars, or throwing a football. We are given gifts. The question is how hard are we willing to work?" Herman said.

John looked at Herman and asked another question. "You told me I should have let you pray. What would have happened if you had?" he asked.

"You may have completed some of those passes." was the only answer Herman could give.

John thought to himself. *"I can't believe I am going to ask a freshman about this, but..."* "Herman do you think we could work together more on the passing end of this game? You have a talent I have not seen in anyone else your age. Normally a 15-year old is still totally a klutz."

Herman gave a little smile and said. "John, the Bible tells us that all good gifts come from above. The question is this - what are we going to do with the gifts we have been given? I can see you have a real gift for leadership. You have led the Bulldogs to winning seasons for the last two years. I can see you're getting rattled because I am here. I am only here to help this team win games. I am here to contribute in any way that God our Father through His Son Jesus by His Holy Spirit opens doors to let me. I can tell you this though, if you are humble, God the Father will shine through you. If you're prideful, he will let you fail on your own. My dad has told me over and over the importance of being humble in all that we do."

Jesus sitting at the right hand of God the Father looked over at Thumbnail. "Good work, little one. You passed on the message that God the Father through His Spirit had for John."

Thumbnail smiled and said, "Thank you, my Lord. There is no greater joy than in being your servant."

John smiled. He knew that this kid was something special. He also realized he was not out to take his starting position away from him. John thought of how Coach Erickson had worked with him since his freshman year getting him ready to start as a senior. Now he had to show only one thing – that he was willing to work and accomplish that which he was created to do for such a time as this.

He walked over to Herman again. "Herm, God has used you to show me something here. Please pray for me. I don't know a lot about God, or Jesus for that matter, but whatever it is you have, I want it."

Herman smiled as he asked John one simple question: "Do you know Jesus Christ as your savior?"

"Nope." was all the John could say. "Tell me about Jesus?"

Herman instantly started to pray. Thumbnail, sitting on his shoulder, got a message for him. "Herm, ask him again. Ask him if he even knows who Jesus is?"

"John are you telling me you don't even know who Jesus is?" Herman asked.

"Is he like some sort of cosmic Santa Claus?" John asked.

"Not at all. Jesus is the Son of God. God the Father is the one who made each and every one of us." Herman answered.

"I don't buy it. I think we are all some kind of accident. I think all of this just happened." John retorted with a wave of his hand.

Herman at the end of his wits simply prayed out loud. "Father in heaven, I lift up John to you right now. Show him tonight who you are. Give him no room to wiggle. Show him in a powerful way you are who your Word says you are. In Jesus' name, Amen."

That night when John went home, he talked about the game with his parents and about the prayer that Herman had prayed for him. The rest of the night he felt uneasy. At 10:00 he went into his room closed the door and started to get ready for bed. Suddenly from behind him he heard, "John" in a deep voice he had never heard before. He turned and saw the angel Gabriel dressed in a gold robe that was so bright it made his eyes hurt.

"Who, who are you?" John stuttered in total fear.

"Who do you think I am?" Gabriel asked in return.

"God?"

"Not at all. I am Gabriel. I am not The Great I Am. I am God the Father's chief angel."

"Ahhhhh. I think I am getting the picture here. I think my life has just changed. What is it God wants from me?" John said.

For the next hour Gabriel explained to John who Jesus is and what he had done for all of mankind. John would get a Bible school education in one hour from Gabriel. His parents walked by the room and told him to turn his light out, but his light was not on. It was the glow from Gabriel's robe that lit up the room. John's sleep that night was the most restful he had ever had in his life.

The next morning when John walked into school he had a new spring in his step. That night at practice his passes were all right on target. He did not brag about how great a player he was. Instead, he gave kudos to the team and pointed to heaven on each pass. Herman was smiling through his helmet. His excitement about his new friend felt amazing.

The rest of the season went by quickly. John was the leader God created him to be. Herman saw very little playing time, but he learned a great deal from John's experience as a great quarterback. Herman's field experience came on the junior varsity team as he was able to put into practice all that he was learning from the varsity team.

October turned into November. Herman was involved in small basketball games after school. Herman was about to learn that if you were a jock in a small school you were expected to play every sport.

Bob Clark, the head basketball coach, just happened to walk into the gym as Herman sank a 40-foot basket. He decided to keep watching for a while and was soon amazed at what Herman Mcbrien could do on the basketball court. Time after time, Herman hit the long shot. The coach stood on the sidelines and shook his head at what he was seeing in Herman.

Coach Clark waived to get the attention of Herman. Herman saw him and walked over to see what was going on. "What's up, Coach?" Herman asked.

Coach Clark put his arm around Herman's shoulder. "Mr. Mcbrien, how would you like to play basketball?"

"Coach, I play football."

"So?" responded the coach. "At small schools like this, people are able to play more than one sport."

"Really!?" Herman answered with a question. "You're telling me I can play basketball and baseball as well?"

"Absolutely!" The coach answered.

"Wow! I am sure gonna like it here." Herman said excitedly.

Herman excelled in basketball. However, he was not really excited about the sport. Even as a freshman, he led the team in scoring, yet the game was not his passion. His thought about basketball was that, like baseball, it was the type of game where one player stands out. One player could make the difference between an unbeaten season and just another regular season. Football was the type of game where every team member was needed to accomplish his job for the team to succeed. This made Herman feel great about what he had been able to do with John in his last season at Carlton.

The Great I Am looked over at Peter and said, "Pete, now we are going to see Herman start to come into his own. What his dad Eli was able to do as an individual on the mound was an amazing thing for the folks to see. Yet, what his son Herman is going to accomplish is going to draw people to me in ways that will amaze even you. Whereas, Eli built on his pitching prowess and knew if there was a hit his teammates would back him up, Herman must depend on his teammates for every play of every game."

Herman played baseball in the spring. He was one of the Bulldogs four pitchers. He had a perfect season with no losses. He was not quite as fast a pitcher as his dad was at that point in his life, but he was extremely effective. Despite his baseball success, his passion was still football.

# The First Whole Summer

May came quickly, and his freshman year was over. That summer he found himself getting involved with the youth group from Elim Lutheran church just a few miles from his home. The first Sunday they had attended Elim, Herman was not impressed with the service. Yes, they did have a worship team, but they followed the liturgy of the Lutheran Church, and that was unfamiliar to him. It seemed old-fashioned. However, as they walked out of the church that first Sunday visit, a cute blonde girl stopped him.

"Excuse me," she said. "Aren't you Herman Mcbrien from Carlton?"

"Yup, that's me." he replied. "And who do I have the pleasure of meeting this morning, coming out of this little church?"

With a bright smile, Lucretia Johnson reach out her hand to shake his and said, "I am Lucretia Johnson. I was in your English class last year. You really had some great insights as to what the authors were trying to get across."

His heart was melted by her smile, Herman grabbed her hand to return the shake. Blushing, he said, "It's a pleasure to meet you. Have you attended this church long?"

Just then a boy by the name of Mark Paulson touched his shoulder. "Hey, you're Herman Mcbrien. I played against you when you pitched for Carlton last spring. Look, we play slow pitch softball in the church league here all summer. How would you like to play?"

Herman looked at Lucretia with her cute smile. "They won just about every game last year. This year with you could be even better." she said.

Herman's mom and dad were standing within ear shot. His dad heard everything and knew this would be great for Herman. He gave a little smile and a nod. "I would love to!" Herman responded.

`Mark said, "Great! first practice is Tuesday night. My dad is the coach. Allen over there is our pitcher."

"Outstanding! I will get to play some other positions. It will be fun doing something besides pitching." Herman responded.

Lucretia got a huge grin on her face. The thought when through her mind. *"Herman seems like a really great guy!"* "Herman, we have a youth group meeting tonight. Care to join us?"

Again, Herman looked at his dad. A slight nod gave him the answer he needed. "I would love too. What time?"

"6:30. We start with a bit of contemporary worship, and then have our Bible study. The study is led by Pastor Peterson." she said excitedly

Peter looked at the Father. "Father there seems to be a connection here, but there was with Alli at the beginning of school and for the whole year last year. What is going on?"

"Pete, I have a call on Herman's life. That call is to do some amazing things in sports as well as ministry outside of the game I am going to have him in. Remember what I said about his dad when he was an eleven-year-old? I said I was going to give him a gift that I give to very few people. If he was willing to work hard, I would give him victories that would astound people. I knew when he was young that he would serve me. My son died so that that My Holy Spirit could indwell men. When he walked out of the grave his mission was complete. My Holy Spirit indwells all those who give their lives to me. It is an answer to the prayer my son prayed in the garden just before he went to the cross. These high school years are going to be a lot of fun for Herman. Because of the place I had his parents move to, I am going to have him become the man I created him to be. He will have many young ladies 'fall in love' with him. I am going to protect his heart and use Thumbnail to do it. I have something special for him. Just watch." the Father said.

When Herman arrived back at the farm he had a question for his dad. "Dad, you have been teaching me the guitar ever since I was a little guy. I would love to take one along tonight. Maybe I could help the worship team. Just maybe I could really bring some life to the whole thing."

Eli looked at Herman and said. "Have you heard them play?"

"No." came Herman's quick answer.

"Then maybe, just maybe, you're judging them because they are Lutherans?" Eli stated in a questioning tone.

"I gotcha, Dad." Herman responded. "But, do you think I could take my guitar just in case?"

As his dad dropped Herman off with his guitar, the members of the worship team surrounded him. "You play guitar too?" they asked him. "What other talents do you have that you're not telling us about?"

They went up front to set up and asked Herman to join them on a set. He did, and his ability to rock out blew the band away. The leader, Dawn Chapin, looked at Herman and asked him to join them in leading the worship that night and every night they met thereafter.

That summer would prove to be the best summer of Herman's life. He would experience things with the softball team he never had playing baseball. In baseball, he pitched shutouts. That was not possible in softball. First, he was not pitching. Second, the game was a much more team sport. There was a great deal of hits, and all members of the team had to be able to do their part to win. Herman found that being able to throw a rocket from the outfield to home plate was a valuable tool. He also found out just how important base running became to the game of softball.

Having earned his driver's license, he was now able to drive himself over to the church. His first night at practice he was surprised by Lucretia being there. As it turned out she had to drive her little brother Soren to practice.

Herman walked to the plate for his first at bat. It was not like playing baseball. The ball came in much more slowly. It was like hitting a change-up all the time. His first pitch he drove out of the field. The diamond was in the back of the church cemetery. It was not a real ball park, but it would do.

After practice Lucretia walked over to Herman. "You are really good. Your first at bat you drove the ball clear across the road into the next pasture." She tried to slip her hand into his.

"Lucretia, I don't think I want this to go in that direction. God is calling me to something and I am not sure what it is. Let's just be friends." Herman said

Lucretia got a stunned look on her face. She was a beautiful girl. She was well liked in school and Herman Mcbrien just wanted to be friends! Everyone at Carlton coupled up, yet Herman did not want to. God the Father was calling him to something. But what? What was it? She was really wondering.

"Pete, he's getting it. He has some amazing things to accomplish, both on the field and off it. He feels my calling in his heart. He knows that allowing things to go beyond friendship with any young lady at this point in his life could throw a wrench into the calling, but he is going to find out I do create a lot of beautiful people.

Over the summer, the Elim Lutheran softball team went undefeated. Herman hit fifteen home runs. Three of them inside the park. He decided that softball was a lot more fun to play than baseball.

One Tuesday night in July, after a tough game they won against Sandy Lake Baptist, the whole team decided to go for a swim. Herman walked in the house to grab his swim trunks and then headed back to the Johnsons' house to pick up Lucretia. She jumped in the passenger door and slid over beside Herman. Her little brother Soren jumped in the passenger door beside her.

They drove the four miles to Sandy Lake. They arrived at the lake and all jumped out of the car. Herman dropped his pants to reveal very conservative boxer swim trunks. Lucretia dropped her terrycloth cover to reveal a bikini that made Herman do a double take. The feeling he was experiencing was not something he had felt before. He turned and headed up the road praying as he walked. "*Jesus help me. I want to be able to treat her with all the honor that you want me to. Give me strength.*"

With that he turned and ran into the water where the rest of the gang was. He dove into the lake and swam out to the raft where the rest of the group was lying in the sun. He climbed up and stretched out to let the warm July sun bake him for a bit. He closed his eyes for just a second and opened them.

Lucretia was standing over him. "You like?" she asked.

Herman stood up. His 6-foot frame was 6 inches taller than Lucretia. "Look, Lucretia, you are a very beautiful child of the king. All through the years my parents have never been afraid to show affection toward each other in front of me. But you know what? Their first kiss was on their wedding day. My grandpa got my dad to promise that he would not kiss her until their wedding and he did not. To be honest, I find you extremely attractive. You in that bikini are really smokin'. My question to you is this though: do you want a guy who wants you for your hot body? Or do you want a guy who really wants to get to know you?"

Lucretia did not answer immediately. Instead she walked to the edge of the raft and dove in and swam to shore. She put on her terry cloth cover, hopped on an inflatable raft, and floated back out to the raft. She climbed on the raft, walked over to Herman, and asked, "Does this answer your question?"

They lay on the raft next to each other for the better part of an hour, simply talking, and sharing their dreams and ambitions. They looked up at the puffy clouds with the blue sky as a back drop. The friendship they started building that day would last a lifetime.

Thumbnail sat on Herman's shoulder and said, "It will be worth it!"

Herman smiled to himself. He did not know where that came from, but he knew it was true.

Lucretia and Herman took the inflatable back to shore. Lucretia put her covering back on and they went for a walk. "Herman, I have never met anyone like you in my life. The respect and control you have is an amazing thing. Do you think...?"

Herman shook his head. "Look, Lucretia, your goal is to study pre-law at Gustavus. Mine is to play Division 1 football and get a degree in business for after my football career is over. We are going in two different directions. Let's enjoy high school and not worry about what happen when it is done. God the Father through His Son by His Holy Spirit will show us both where he wants us."

Lucretia got a quizzical look on her face. "Really? That's what you think?" she asked.

At that second Thumbnail whispered in her ear. "It will be worth the wait."

Lucretia looked around herself. "Who said that?" she asked.

"Look, Lucretia, I know we are not designed to be together forever. God has someone special for you and for me. It's just not each other. One thing I have noticed at Carlton is couples pairing up. They think they have "fallen in love," but the problem is they don't even know what love looks like. When you meet the person that God the Father through his Son Jesus by His Holy Spirit has for you, there will be an electric charge that you will not be able to deny. High school relationships tend to be status symbols. I don't want to be anyone's status symbol." Herman stated.

Thumbnail gleefully jumped up and down on Lucretia's shoulder so much she could almost feel him.

Lucretia looked at Herman. Herman looked back into her deep blue eyes. He knew there was a strong attraction there. Yet, he also knew that he would never act on it. At least he thought he would never act on it. As they stood on the side of the road that went around Sandy Lake, he wondered if he would be as strong as his dad. "*Mom had to be a huge turn on for dad when they were dating. Dad stayed true to his promise. I have seen how attracted they are to each other to this day.*" He smiled at Lucretia and turned and looked up to heaven. "Father how can I do this?" was all he asked.

The Father looked at Pete. "Make sure Thumbnail knows that there may be trouble down the road. When Eli and Jill were dating he kept them out of a lot of trouble. Herman can't allow himself to get to that position. We must protect him from himself."

When they decided it was time to leave, they yelled to Soren, so they could take him home as well. They had a feeling that if they left him at the lake, Lucretia's mom would not be very happy with them. The conversation in the car on that few mile drive was quite mundane. Soren was trying to figure out what was going on between Lucretia and Herman. Soren being just a year younger and a great admirer of Herman was hoping that they would become a couple. At this point Herman knew what was best. He knew what God had, yet he knew these feeling he had meant something as well. He just did not know for sure what they meant.

When they pulled in the driveway Lucretia told Soren to go in the house. When Soren got into the house their mother asked Soren where she was. He told her that Herman and Lucretia were still "talking" in the car. She walked to the window. She saw Lucretia sitting on one side of the front seat and Herman sitting on the other. She shrugged her shoulders and walked away from the window.

Lucretia asked Herman a question he would hear frequently over the next few years from a lot of the kids at Carlton. "Herman what have you got? I have never seen anyone with as much discipline as you have. If I would have stood over any other guy the way I was standing over you on that raft, I don't know what would have happened. It would probably not have been good. You just stood up and asked me that question, which I had never thought of before. What is it you have?"

Herman smiled as he answered, "Look, Lucretia, I have seen few girls as beautiful as you. No, let me restate that. I have never seen your beauty in anyone. You don't realize what you have. When we first got out of the car and you walked to the lake and dropped your terry cloth, I about dropped my teeth. That's why I turned and started praying. My prayer was that I would be able to treat you with the honor a child of the king deserves. What I have is a close, intimate relationship with my Heavenly Father through His Son Jesus by His Holy Spirit. It's only when we have that relationship that we can be truly free. Would you like to have that totally close relationship with God the Father through His son Jesus by His Holy Spirit?"

Lucretia asked, "What do I have to do to get that relationship?"

Herman replied, "As a Lutheran you were baptized as a baby. At that point, Jesus puts his hand on you and will do everything short of coercion to bring you to himself. There does come a point though when you must choose for yourself who you are going to serve. All you have to do is ask."

"Can you help me?" Lucretia asked Herman.

With that, Herman took her hands in his and led her in a prayer of power and submission to God the Father through His Son by His Holy Spirit.

Lucretia looked at Herman and said, "I suppose I should get in."

Herman responded, "Let me walk you to the door."

Herman got out of the car, walked around, and opened Lucretia's door for her. They walked to the door and stood there for a second looking into each other's eyes.

"Can friends hug?" Lucretia asked.

"Sure." Herman responded.

Lucretia put her arms around Herman's neck and hugged him tightly. She then kissed him on the cheek. "That, my friend, was a holy kiss."

Herman turned a little red and said thank you. Lucretia opened the door and went inside. Herman stood there on the porch. He put his hand on his cheek where Lucretia had kissed him. He looked up to heaven and simply asked. "Father, help. The feelings I have for this girl are so strong, and I barely even know her. Help."

Thumbnail whispered to him. "Don't worry, Father has everything under control."

Herman turned walked back to the car, got in, and drove home.

Peter looked at the Father and asked a question. "Father, you know everything, I thought this was going to be a life-long friendship. What is their life-long friendship going to look like?"

The Father looked back at Peter and said. "Pete, you know that I won't tell you that."

Pete smiled. "I know, I just thought maybe..."

From that mid-July day on the raft until the 15th of August, Lucretia and Herman went for long walks and spent many hours talking. There was no physical contact, just a lot of deep conversation. There was Bible study and there was prayer. When they said goodbye there was a hug, but nothing else. The friendship grew and grew. They built a strong intellectual and emotional tie as they spent more and more time together. Yet, they both knew it would end when the summer would end – or so they thought.

# Jim Erickson

AUGUST 15TH CAME AROUND SOONER than Herman wanted it to. Monday morning was the first morning of two-a-days. He had to be at practice by 7:30. They didn't need to suit up or wear pads. There were just intense, gut-wrenching wind sprints. The morning started with push-ups and stretches. Coach Erickson walked through the ranks of players demanding their best. Just as before, he was getting them ready for the last two minutes of every game. Herman knew what he had to do. And, yes! He had Thumbnail on his shoulder, just like when his dad was getting ready for the season in baseball. Herman ran, sprinted, and worked extremely hard. He knew his role as the leader of this team required that he be in top shape. He did not know what each game would demand of him, but he did know he would be ready for it.

After practice he would practically crawl into the locker room. He had to be able to handle the work out. He had to be in shape. But after practice he was exhausted.

The evening practice was much lighter than the morning one. The team started to work on some passing plays.

Herman was able to get his receivers out at 50 yards and put the ball softly right into their hands.

Little did he know that Lucretia had driven into town to watch him. She was standing a way off with the other girl friends of the other players.

After practice Herman was walking towards the locker room when he heard, "Herm, great practice!" being yelled at him from a distance. He turned and saw Lucretia and waved at her.

Just then Coach Erickson tapped Herman on the shoulder. "Herman, you're my best quarterback. I don't want you getting distracted by a cute girl and getting your attention off football." he said with a wink.

"We're just friends!" Herman responded.

John Smith, the center on the team, looked at Herman. "Herm, you better look at how she looks at you. She wants more than friendship."

Herman thought. *"That's the problem. I think I do to."*

The Father looked at Peter. "Get Thumbnail on this one. They have freedom of choice, but choices have consequences. This will not end well if they choose wrongly."

Thumbnail jumped on Herman's shoulder as Herman was thinking about Lucretia. "Herman, end this now. It will not end well if you don't." Thumbnail warned him.

Pete looked at the Father. "Father, what do you mean when you say, it will not end well? Does something terrible happen between them?"

"No, not at all. People make choices without thinking. I can't tell you what is going to happen. Let's just see if Herman will listen to Thumbnail."

Herman looked at Lucretia who had come up to him. "Give me fifteen minutes to take a shower. Then we can go over to the Dairy Queen and get an ice cream cone."

Herman came out showered and dressed. He walked over to Lucretia and suddenly got a cramp in his right thigh that made him jump up and down to try get it to release. After five minutes of excruciating pain, he finally got the muscle to release. Then they hopped in the old pickup truck his dad had bought for work on the farm and for Herman to use for running back and forth to school for practice and headed over to the Dairy Queen.

Memories flooded Herman's mind of all the times his dad took him to Lipinski's Dairy Queen for Blizzards after his Little League games back in California. He drove down the streets of Carlton with a huge smile on his face.

Lucretia asked, "What are you smiling about?"

"Nothing much really. Just a memory of another Dairy Queen that my dad used to take us to after a game back in California."

Lucretia, not one to be denied, pressed him a bit. "Care to share with me a bit of that great time?"

"I was eleven and had just won my first game. I wanted to go to Lipinski's Dairy Queen. Tom, the owner, was a close friend of my dad, so I kinda just threw it out there. My dad said sure, and we went to Lipinski's." Herman shared.

Lucretia was sitting beside him in the truck. She was such a beautiful young lady, and Herman was starting to have some strong feelings for this girl who was so sweet and interested in him.

"Herman you need to end this. You need to break up with her." Herman shook his head.

Then he suddenly blurted out, "No way!"

Lucretia got a strange look on her face. "What?" she asked.

"Oh, it's nothing really." Herman said, turning a little red in the face

The next Monday at early practice they started working on plays. Herman was totally focused on what he was doing. His passes were right on the money. After practice, he drove home, and his mom had a huge breakfast waiting for him, which he scarfed down in record time.

Eli came in off the tractor. "Hey, Bud! How was practice?"

"Dad, it was great. I'll be starting against Esko. They usually clean our clocks, but not this year. We have it all together. We will win this game!" He paused and then continued, "Hey, Dad, can we go for a walk? There is something I want to talk to you about."

Herman and Eli walked out of the house and headed down towards the pond. "What is it, Son?" Eli asked.

"You know that little voice you told me you heard when you were on the mound?" Herman asked.

"Yeah?" Eli responded.

"Well, Dad, I think I am hearing him." Herman said.

"What about?" Eli questioned.

"Well, Dad, it's like this. I have met this great girl at Elim Lutheran. She goes to my school too. Her name is Lucretia Johnson. She's smart, sweet, and smoking hot."

"Ah!" Eli responded. "Son, is she a believer?"

Thumbnail jumped on Eli's shoulder. "Eli, he needs to break up with her." The little angel said with great authority.

Herman spoke with total confidence. "Dad she asked what I had. I told her it was a close intimate relationship with Jesus Christ. She told me she wanted that. We prayed on the spot and she accepted Christ."

"Son, did she pray that because that is what she wanted, or did she pray that because she wanted to get close to you?" Eli asked quietly. "Herman I just heard the same voice you did. God's messenger spoke with an authority that I have not heard often. He told me what I think he may have told you. You should break up with her."

"Dad I can't. I just can't. I don't understand this whole thing yet, but right now I just can't."

"Okay, Son. I think this could be a disaster waiting to happen, but okay."

They walked back to the house. Herman hopped into the truck and went back to practice. That afternoon, Herman was once again totally focused. His passes were spot on every time. He knew what every man on the team had to do, and he could call an audible at the drop of a hat. He could see a linebacker not where he should be and take advantage of it every time.

This went on all week. At night his focus was on his play book. He knew what he was gifted to do, and he was going to do it.

Friday's game arrived quickly. The game was being played on Esko's home turf. Carlton came on the field to warm up and the first thing the Bulldogs noticed was how fit the boys from Esko were. On the first set of downs, Herman dropped back to pass and a big farm boy from Esko was right on top of him. Herman quickly turned left and scrambled, looking down field. He spotted Kevin Derusha wide open and hit him right in the hands. Touch down! Herman did not see it, however, as he was laid out by the big farm boy from Esko.

It was a high scoring game, but Carlton's speed did prove to be too much for Esko. Carlton won by a slim three points. When they got back to the locker room, Herman had to sit in the hot whirlpool tub for nearly an hour just to get his sore muscles limber enough, so he could walk back to his truck. But starting the season with a win against Esko was a big boost to the Bulldogs and Herman.

When Herman finally limped out to the parking lot, Lucretia was waiting for him. She looked at him as if he were a wounded warrior. She met him at his truck and asked if he was going to go hangout with the team at The Junction.

Herman could hardly walk. He smiled weakly and said, "Not tonight. I hurt all over. Let's touch base in the morning."

Eli drove the family car up to the door of the locker room. "Herm, you okay, man?"

"Dad, I hurt all over. I have never been beaten up like that before. We got the win, but they sure made us pay a price to get it." Herman said. He stumbled to his truck and drove home.

The next morning, Herman woke to the sun shining in his bright yellow bedroom. "Whose idea was it to paint this room canary yellow? When it's cloudy it's bright. When it's sunny, this room is so bright my eyes hurt." Herman started to get up out of bed and quickly stopped short. Every bone, every muscle hurt. He started to head for the stairs to go down. His legs cramped up so tight he screamed. Eli came running up the stairs. "What's going on son?" he asked with concern in his voice.

"Dad, I have never hurt this much. Every inch of my body is sore. I have never been pounded like I was last night. I have no idea how I am going to get ready for Wrenshall next week.

"Son, the first thing you're going to do is get your trunks on and climb into the hot tub. Then we will see what you feel like."

Just then the phone rang. Jill answered the phone. Then she brought it up to Herman in his room. "Hi Lu. What's up? Me? I can hardly move. Dad is going to help me to the new hot tub he had installed on the patio. Do I want company?" He looked at his mom and dad who both nodded their approval. "Yeah, that would be great. By the time I can get my trunks on and down these stairs you should be here. Ok, see ya soon."

Herman was able to slowly work his way down the stairs. The soreness from the beating he had taken the previous night on the football field was evident. The one thought on his mind, however, was Lucretia joining him in the hot tub for some Christ-centered conversation. As he hobbled into the dining room he saw his breakfast on the table. Bacon, eggs, and pancakes were sitting on his plate. "Mom, I think

I could use a cup of coffee this morning." he said as he sat at the table.

As Jill poured his coffee she said, "Man, last night you were a half a second ahead of those linemen."

All Herman could do was nod. His body was reminding him of the game he had played the night before. The one thing he could not deny was how hungry he was. He devoured his breakfast just as Lucretia came up the driveway.

Lucretia hopped out of her car, smiling as she walked to the house. She was wearing her terry cloth cover. She walked into the house and greeted Herman's mom and dad. She then sat at the table across from Herman and said cheerfully, "Good morning!"

The Father looked over at Gabriel. "Tonight, you give him a dream. In that dream you show him the importance of him ending the relationship on its current course. These kids will serve me, but not as one. I have roles for them that go in totally different directions." the Father said.

Herman looked at his parents. He got up from the table and winced in pain. He moved very gingerly out to the hot tub. Lucretia walked with him, her heart breaking with every flinch he made. As they reached the hot tub, Herman carefully climbed in. "This feels soooo good." He said with a huge sigh of relief.

Herman looked over as Lucretia removed her terrycloth cover. To his pleasant surprise she was wearing a much more conservative one-piece swimsuit. He could not help but smile as she said, "I took to heart what you said at Sandy Lake. I realized that we are created for other people. At this point in our lives we don't know who that person is. It is important that we keep ourselves pure for that love of our lives, but to be honest, Herm, I still really like you." She smiled, and Herman's heart started to melt.

They sat in the hot tub for an hour, on opposite sides of the tub. Herman knew in his heart that allowing himself to get physical in any way with this beautiful girl would be the wrong thing to do. He really wanted to, but he would not allow himself to do that.

After relaxing in the hot tub, his muscles and joints were feeling much better. Eli walked up to the tub. "Okay, you two. I need to get some help here. Herman take a look at those bales of hay laying out in the fields. I am going to drive the tractor and you will throw them up and then climb up and stack them."

Herman smiled and said, "I knew there was a reason you wanted me in the tub to loosen up. You had motives."

Lucretia grinned and chimed in, "Look, you two, I have clothes in my car. Why don't I get changed and drive the tractor? That way one of you can be on the trailer and the other one can throw the bales up. That way you can get this done much faster."

"Sounds good to me." Eli said. "Let's get to work.

They spent the next three hours picking up hay bales. The more bales Herman threw, the less he hurt. By the time they were done, he was feeling loose and limber and ready for practice on Monday.

At 4:30 Herman looked down the driveway to see Coach Erickson driving up. He got out of the car walked up to where Herman, Eli, and Lucretia were standing, having just unloaded the tractor. "How is my star quarterback?" he asked.

"Doing okay, Coach." Herman replied.

"Good. I have a new set of plays that I think may make your job a little easier." He handed Herman the new play and told him to have it ready by Monday.

Coach said his goodbyes and headed back to his car. The real reason he had wanted to see Herman was to make sure he was alright after the beating he had taken at Esko the night before.

Eli walked up to Herman. "Son, Lucretia worked really hard today. I think you ought to take her to a nice dinner at a nice restaurant. Here's some money. Go enjoy yourselves."

Herman walked over to Lucretia and told her what his dad had said. She smiled, walked over to Eli, and said,

"Thank you, Mr. Mcbrien. This means a lot." She then went home to get ready for the evening.

The night was magical. Herman picked Lucretia up promptly at 6:30. They went to The Junction for a nice dinner, and then they walked along the St. Louis River. Herman really wanted to take her hand as they walked and talked. He knew in his heart of hearts though that this was something he should not do. And the little voice of Thumbnail kept telling him not too. At one point, as they were walking towards a park next to the river, they turned and looked into each other's eyes. The glow of the city lights shining on Lucretia's face made her look so pure and angelic Herman wanted to kiss her.

"Don't do it." Thumbnail whispered in his ear. Instantly back in the Father's presence, Thumbnail told the Father that this job with Herman was much harder than it ever was with Eli.

The Father smiled as he said, "Well, Eli made a promise to Jill's dad. He had the integrity to not break a promise. Herman has not made that promise. The dream we have planned for Herman will show just him how much love he has for her. A person who truly loves another person is willing to walk away from that other person if it is the best for the other person. Real love means being willing to make sacrifices for the betterment of the other."

Herman looked at the beautiful Lucretia. He suggested they walk back to the car. He needed to get home and look over the play book.

Lucretia looked at him and asked sweetly. "Pick me up Monday for school?"

His answer was matter of fact. "I'll see what time I actually get my butt out of bed." He opened her door, went around, got in the car and drove her home.

The conversation from Cloquet back to her house was most enjoyable. Being the perfect gentleman, once they arrived at Lucretia's house, Herman walked around, opened her door, and walked her to the house.

Lucretia got a sly grin on her face as she said, "Can friends hug?"

Herman smile as he opened his arms to Lucretia. The hug was long and tight, and as they separated Lucretia kissed Herman on the cheek. She said goodnight and went into the house.

Herman walked to the car drinking in the warm early September night. He got in and drove the five miles home.

As he walked into the house Eli could see something was wrong written all over his face. "Son, what's the problem?" Eli asked.

"Dad, I really can't explain it. Lucretia is amazing. She is beautiful and smart. We talked about the Lord for a solid two hours as we walked along the river in Cloquet. I just don't know. Why would God the Father not want us together?" Herman asked.

Eli shrugged his shoulder and replied, "Why don't you ask him?"

Herman looked at his dad and responded by telling him he had to study the play book for practice Monday. He went to his room picked up the play book and started going over the new counter plays. He sat on his bed and set the play book down beside him. Restlessly, he got up off his bed walked around the room and started asking God the Father through the Son by the Holy Spirit why he was not supposed to get serious with Lucretia. He named off all her great characteristics. He couldn't think of any bad ones. He truly wanted to know what the Father's mind really was on this. He walked over to his bed, took off his shoes, opened his play book, and read it as he laid on his back.

As he was committing to his mind every assignment for the new counter plays, he fell into a deep sleep. The play book slid onto the floor. He was dreaming. *He was outside of Lucretia's house. She came out in a beautiful wedding dress. She walked to the waiting car and got into the back seat. He found himself in the backseat with her whole wedding party. They were headed to the church for the wedding. He could hear the excitement in her voice as she talked about the future they would have together. He looked on beauty of her face. Her shining eyes. The slight turns up of her noise. Then he heard a horn. He saw a truck being driven by a drunk driver crash into Lucretia's door. She was killed instantly.*

Herman woke screaming, "**Noo! Nooo!**"

His mom and dad came rushing to the room. "Herm, what's going on?" his dad asked with alarm.

Herman with tears running down his cheeks kept saying, "She's dead. I know she's dead."

Eli looked at his son who was distressed in a way he had never seen before. "Herman, you were dreaming. Let me pray for you." Eli then prayed for the peace that passes all understanding, and Herman was able to go back to sleep and sleep the rest of the night in peace.

The next morning Herman made up his mind that he could not allow his relationship with Lucretia to go beyond friendship. No matter how much he cared for her, he was willing to let her go completely. He decided to heed the warnings that had being given to him. He knew that he would have a life-long friendship with this lovely child of the King named Lucretia, but that is all it would ever be.

The Father smiled as he said. "Now I can use Herman. Now I know what level of love he is capable of. He was willing to give up someone he loves to make sure that she can be all that I have created her to be. You see, I have plans for each of them. They are both going to be part of my purpose. I am going to use them both at Carlton over the next few years to build a legacy of truth and holiness that will go on for many years."

Peter looked at the Father with a look of total confusion. "Father, if they are going to have such a huge impact on this school as friends, why not have them marry and continue that role?"

The Father chuckled as he said. "Peter, I have my reasons for all that I do. I am training these kids to be powerful tools in my arsenal. They will be mighty warriors for my kingdom. I will use them to destroy the enemy of people's souls. They both have over seventy years left on the earth. What you see between them is a genuine love for me, and for each other. Love like theirs between two people does not always lead to marriage, but it always leads to people being drawn to my love and compassion. Watch what I do with their lives."

That Sunday in church Herman and Lucretia sat together, enjoying the traditional service. Herman like to worship in the traditional service and then in the following hour he joined the band to play music in the contemporary service. He and Lucretia team-taught the younger kids with great excitement too.

The younger kids were excited to listen to Herman and Lucretia. Afterall, how many kids could say they were taught by a great quarterback who could run a Sunday school class much like he did a huddle or a game?

Sunday ended too quickly, and Monday came too soon. Herman picked up Lucretia on their way to school for their first day of their sophomore year. As they walked in, Alli came running up to Eli. "Hi! How are you doing?" she asked, excited to see her friend.

Herman with his broad smile answered. "I am doing really great. I had a great summer. How about you?"

Alli with her electric smile said," My summer was amazing." Then she looked at Lucretia. "Are you two a couple?".

Lucretia laughed. "We have developed a great friendship. We have decided that's where it stays. We both feel we can be used by our Father in heaven better if we keep it there."

Just then the warning bell rang for the first hour. "Alli why don't you join us for lunch? We must get things rolling for the new student believer's fellowship we are going to start this year. We could use your input." Lucretia said.

The Father was giddy as he said. "I have put something wonderful together. I have three kids who, even while being underclassmen, are going to quickly become leaders because of the personalities that I have developed in them for such a time as this. It is a rare and beautiful thing when three kids can come together for common cause of my gospel like this. Peter, the fun is about to start. Watch as these kids really take off, and watch my purpose be established in Carlton High School.

After school Herman walked into the locker room. One of his linemen, Joe, walked up to him. "So, Herm, dating two girls at once. How's that work?"

Herman had to control the anger he suddenly felt towards this buffoon. He walked up to the bigger guy, stood nose to nose with him, and said, "Look, Joe, those two young ladies are great friends. They are also God's princesses. You will please refrain from any negative statements about them."

Joe being a bit of a bully pushed on. "What if I don't? What if I call them what they are?"

Before Herman could answer Coach, Erickson stepped in. "Joe, there's the door. You're done. This team must be united. I don't need guys taking on other players. I need team members who supports each other."

Joe looked at the coach and asked for a second chance. Coach Erickson looked at Joe, then at Herman. Herman smiled walked over to Joe and asked if he would like to help with a project they were working on.

Joe looked at Herman, then Coach Erickson. Coach Erickson said, "Joe, you have to prove to me that you are willing to be a real teammate. I know what project they are working on. I know these three are doing something great for everyone who is willing to take part in what they are doing. Here's the deal. You take part, help them out. Get to know these young ladies for who they are. Don't miss any blocks and protect your quarterback in every game. You can play."

"Peter, I now have the team put together. These four kids are going to be great workers in my kingdom. Not just now, but for years to come. Herman and Joe are going to be great friends. I am going to put them together not only for high school football, but they will play together in college as well. I am going to even have them play in the pros together." the Father said.

Herman and Joe met up the following morning. Lucretia and Allie joined them. Joe was about to see what true friendships were all about. He was about to see what working together for a common goal meant. And most importantly, he was going to find out how Jesus the Christ would change his life forever.

Joe could see the way that Lucretia and Herman looked at each other. He thought it strange that they only wanted to keep what was going on between them as a friendship. After lunch Joe pulled Herman aside to ask him about it. "Herman, how can you just be friends with Lucretia? It's clear you both want more, why not go for it?"

Herman shook his head as he said, "Joe, it's like this. God works with eternal things. He looks way beyond where we are at now. We both honor marriage. We both know that we will be going in opposite directions after high school. We both know that the plans our Father in heaven has for us don't include each other. Don't get me wrong. To be with Lucretia would be an amazing thing, and it will for the one God the Father has chosen for her. It's not me. God chose my mom and dad for each other early in their lives. They met in high school. He has not done so for us. We both know this must remain a friendship and nothing more."

Joe shook his head. He could not get his brain wrapped around what Herman was saying. He had always looked on girls as objects or play things, something to be taken advantage of for his own selfish pleasure. To develop friendships was something that he had not even thought of doing. "*How does a guy just be friends with girls as hot as Lucretia and Allie?*"

Thumbnail perched on his shoulder spoke clearly to him. "Joe, it's like this. Those two girls are children of the Most High, the Great I Am. They are pure and holy before God the Father. God has placed you in front of them to be their protector. You are to be a friend, and you are to make sure that anyone who would have bad intentions towards them does not even get close. As you protect Herman's blind side on the football field, you will protect their purity off of it. Is that clear?"

Joe shook his head and looked around himself. He was about to put the whole thing out of his mind, but he turned around and saw Gabriel standing there, all ten feet of him. "I understand," was all he could say.

"Good." Gabriel said and vanished.

During Friday's game, Herman had an easy time passing to his wide-open receivers. As he he dropped back to pass, Wrenshall's defensive lineman started to rush, but on his left side, that lineman got crushed by Joe protecting Herman's blindside. Carlton won the game 65-3. After the game the four friends went to The Junction to get something to eat.

Herman drove Joe out to meet the girls at the diner. As they arrived the found a very disturbing scene. The girls were trying to get into The Junction, but a couple of jerks were giving them a rough time. Herman and Joe walked up to the boys who were bothering the girls. "Is there a problem here?" Joe asked.

The Father looked at Peter with a slight grin on his face. "Pete, watch this. Thumbnail and Gabriel made a huge impact on Joe today. Those two young boys who don't know me yet are going find out what kind of Hell gets delivered on those who come against my kids."

"These guys are coming onto us in the most sexual ways they could think of. They have been talking to us like they think we are cheap whores." Alli exclaimed with disgust.

The 6'4" Joe walked up to Tim, the one who had been harassing Alli. "Tim, I think you owe the lady an apology."

"For what calling her what she is?" Tim replied snottily.

Joe with a slight chuckle put his arm around Tim's shoulder. "Listen, Tim. If you do not apologize right now, you will be sorry for the day you were born."

Tim not wanting to seem like a coward replied, "Never happen."

Herman was standing beside Lucretia as the scene unfolded. Lucretia leaned over to Herman and asked, "Aren't you going to stop this?"

Herman chuckled as he answered, "Not a chance. He is about to learn a lesson that may save his life later."

Thumbnail was fluttering right at Joe's ear as he said. "Joe, pick Tim up by the neck. Tell him that Jesus said it would be better for a man to have a millstone tied around his neck than cause one of his little ones to stumble. You're causing Alli to stumble. You have two choices. Don't apologize and taste the wrath of God through me or apologize and slink out of here like the snake that you are."

The cowardly Tim turned white as Joe repeated what Thumbnail told him to say. He started to sweat with fear then finally said, "Okay. I will apologize."

Joe let him down. Tim sheepishly faced Alli and apologized to her before running away.

Alli walked over to Joe. "Thank you." she said, looking up at him with a tear in her eyes that totally broke his heart.

Big Joe knew something important was happening. What he did not understand was what Alli had that he did not. He asked her," What have you got? There is something about you I do not understand. It has such a powerful draw."

The 5'2" Alli turned her face up to Big Joe said, "It's Jesus! It's the Holy Spirit of God himself. You need God more than you know."

"Let's go inside and eat." Big Joe said. He was famished.

For the next two hours Alli, Herm, and Lucretia were able to share with Big Joe all that Christ had done for them. They were able to explain to Joe the reality of who Christ really is. Joe was transfixed by it all. What blew him away was the idea of purity in friendships. He was coming to an understanding that by looking at each other as a true child of the king these kids did not want to have their relationships be reduced to pure animalistic lust. He came to understand that by following the scriptural guide for every part of his life that he would come to understand that children of the king were all special, and building a true, long-lasting relationship required building a friendship that could not be broken.

After they had finished their burgers and fries, Herman and Big Joe walked the girls back to their car. Big Joe stood towering over Alli and did not know exactly what to do to say goodbye. He fumbled awkwardly trying to figure out what to do. He thought to himself. *"I can crush a linebacker trying to get to my quarterback, why can't I figure out what to do here."*

Allie figured out the problem Big Joe was having. "Just hug me goodbye. "she said.

Big Joe reached down and gave Allie a big hug and smiled.

Allie looked back with a radiant smile and said. "Bye. See you in school on Monday."

Big Joe drew a deep breath and asked, "May I call you?"

Allie replied. "I would be disappointed if you didn't."

Practice that week was brutal. Coach Erickson demanded perfection from the team. But they were ready for anything that would happen in the game against Cromwell that Friday because of that week's practice.

Coach Erickson had made them run the counter-pass repeatedly. It felt like a hundred times, but when they ran it in the game, Todd Benson was wide open in the end-zone, and Herman laid the ball in so softly a baby could catch it, the crowd went wild.

Carlton's defense totally stymied Cromwell. They could not run the ball or pass it. They were stuffed on each possession. After the game the Bulldogs went out on the field for their victory chant. "Gubba, gubba, gubba, ha ha ha." Over and over again. Herman and his team were experiencing a huge emotional release after the hard week of practice that ended with a score of 56-0 – another shut out for the defense.

If there was one-person Herman looked up to it was Coach Jim Erickson. The coach would not compromise on doing the right thing. He would do things that may embarrass a player in the short term but have long lasting positive effects for the rest of that player's life. He always wanted his teams to win, but not at the cost of good sportsmanship. Coach Erickson was a coaches' coach.

Having won the Polar League with a perfect season Herman realized the daunting challenge before the whole team. They would be expected to repeat the same results for the next two seasons. Before that could happen, he needed to finish the rest of the school year, and that meant basketball and baseball seasons, and other extra-curricular activities. Amid all these activities he found himself with two-real loves. One that he would be able to attack with a vigor that would make things happen for him and give him a platform for all that God was preparing for him. That was football. The other was a young lady that he knew God wanted to be his friend. Herman was starting to feel like he understood why God the Father through His Son by His Holy Spirit wanted them to have a close friendship and not a romance.

Peter looked at the Father of all mankind asked, "Father, why is it that you have Lucretia and Herman being only friends? There seems to such an attraction there. Is it not possible that you could create something really powerful between those two?"

"I could Pete, but it's not my best. My best is created over time. I put the right people together for hundreds if not thousands of years to get the perfect mix of DNA so that the person I create for the calling I have on their lives is equipped the best they can be to accomplish the greatest they possibly can with the time I give them on the earth. Let's look at Jill, for instance. I started creating her at the time of the Revolutionary War. Her great-great-great grandfather was a general in the war. I needed to pass on to her the quick decision making necessary in a war to be passed onto

Herman for him to be able to react to any situation on a football field. Someday when he is coaching, he will be able to pass onto high school boys the same type of things. Not at his high level, but he can help them be the most effective with the gifts I have engineered in them."

Pete looked at the Father and said, "I think I am getting it."

The Father continued. "Pete, think of a surgeon who can operate on a baby in its mother's womb. I am more than willing to spend the time necessary to create the perfect surgeon. I may take twenty generations to create the person I want, but I will get that person created. That's why I put so much emphasis in my word about the importance of using one's talents to accomplish as much as one can with those talents. I bring people together to accomplish what is best for all concerned."

Pete looked at the Father and asked one more question. "Father, what happens when folks get together out of pure lust?"

"Pete, all things work together for good for those who love me and are called according to my purpose. I have some dynamic people working in my kingdom who were created in less than perfect circumstances. When anyone turns to me, I can do amazing things. What I am talking about here is my planning of individuals over centuries to accomplish pure, undeniable greatness. I can use some interesting situations to create amazing people. In this case with Lucretia and

Herman, I have wonderful things planned for them, just not with each other. However,"

"However, what?" Peter asked.

"Stay tuned." The Father said smiling.

As Herman walked into school the Monday after the end of the football season, Lucretia came walking up to Herman with a big smile on her face. "So, tell me, Herm, what are you going to do in speech this year?"

"Speech?" Herman answered.

"Yup. If you're going to get picked up by a Division 1 school, you really need to have a well-rounded education." Lucretia stated with a sly grin.

Herman looked at his dear friend Lucretia and stated emphatically, "I don't even like speech. It is not my thing. I don't want to do it."

"Herman let's say you end up playing big time football. You will have thousands upon thousands of fans chasing after you. You can be the man God our Father has created you to be and be able to speak to those folks comfortably because you started preparing for it in high school, or you can look like you forgot how to speak at all when you find yourself in front of a crowd." Lucretia said in a rather motherly tone.

Herman was shaking his head. "I think I am going to go talk to Mrs. Allen about getting on the speech team. I also know this. If I am going to do something I am going all out. This should be interesting." Herman said.

Pete smiled. "Father you have a way of using women in guys lives to get them to do what you need them to do, don't you?"

The Father simply smiled. He needed to say nothing. The answer was obvious.

Herman went to Mrs. Allen's room to talk to her about the speech team. When he walked in, she looked up from her desk and smiled at him. "Herman Mcbrien. There were times when my late husband, even while sick, would get so excited watching your dad play baseball. Seeing Eli Mcbrien strike out batter after batter seemed to give my husband a thrill that nothing else could. In the last World Series your dad played in, my husband only had a few weeks left to live. He was weak, but seeing the strength seem to come back to him. He would holler and yell at the TV. The doctor told me to let him enjoy the games. Two weeks after your dad got his last win in the series against Minnesota my husband was gone. Just know this. Your dad gave my late husband a thrill that I'll remember the rest of my life."

Herman could not help but smile. "Yeah, I guess my dad is a pretty special guy. I just hope I can be half the man he is. Mrs. Allen, I am here because a friend of mine says I should get on the speech team. She said it would help me later as God uses me in football. What do you think I should do?"

Mrs. Allen got a smile on her face. "Would you rather make people laugh or cry?" She asked.

"Laugh, of course." Herman answered.

Mrs. Allen handed him a very funny piece to read. It was a piece from *God: The Ultimate Autobiography* by Jeremy Pascall. Herman started reading through it and began to laugh and kept laughing until he cried. "I have to do this!" he said.

Smiling, Mrs. Allen walked over to him and told him to memorize the piece and have it ready to start working on by Monday. Herman looked at the piece. He figured it to have about eight hundred words that he would need to memorize. He thought of the weekend he had planned with Lucretia. Then it hit him. "*I'll get her to help me.*".

"Pete, you are about to see what I do with people at a young age to get them ready for tremendous things later. It does little good for me to give gifts to a young person for them to have a platform, and then not be able to use that platform to accomplish some pretty great things. When I get a young person to build one talent upon another they can be the complete servant that will receive some great rewards both on the earth and when they come into my heavenly kingdom. But for them to accomplish the greatness I have for them, they must be willing to put the work in. Herman, like his dad, is willing to put the work in."

Jesus got a sly grin on his face. "Father, I have come up with a play that I think will make some really big things happen on the football field for Herman. I have sent Thumbnail to whisper it to Coach Erickson in his sleep. If he uses it, we could see some real fireworks."

The next day, Herman was standing by his locker still trying to wake up. Like his dad, he was not a morning person. Coach Erickson saw him standing in the hallway. Walked up to him handed him the new play and said, "This play came to me in my sleep. Now that basketball is over, and we are going into the spring and you start baseball, I thought you may want to have a little fun on the side. I can't formally be at any practices, but look at this, and see what you think."

Herman and Big Joe were standing together with Lucretia and Allie. Herman looked at the play and exclaimed "wow!" as his eyes widened.

Joe got a puzzled look on his face. "Can I see the play?" he asked. Herman handed it to him, and Joe looked at the play "Wow! A triple reverse with a tackle passing the ball to you deep down the right sideline. Is this even legal?"

"I hope you can throw the ball man!" was all Herman could say.

It was March 1st. The snow was still on the ground, and the baseball team was working out in the gym. Herman was throwing the ball at a respectable 85 miles per hour. His control was amazing. The feeling on the team was one of expectation going into the season. Half the team was made up of football players. Big Joe, however, was running track instead. He threw the shot put and the discus and anchored the last leg of the quarter-mile relay. Joe understood the importance of speed if he wanted to play college ball. He had to be fast enough to take out a quick linebacker. In the back of his mind was the triple reverse pass he was looking forward to throwing in the next football season. Every shot he put, every discus he threw, he knew it helped him get closer to throwing the 50-yard pass that he would land in Herman's hands for a touchdown. He could not wait until the fall for football to start.

# The Last Two Years at Carlton

THEIR SOPHOMORE YEAR WAS THE start of Carlton's best three years in sports ever. It was the year when they started to accomplish real greatness. In their junior and senior years, they would achieve greatness that would never be matched at Carlton again. This little school would prove to be a powerhouse for a couple of years. But the real power would come from the Holy Spirit working in students as they were drawn to the love of God that Herman and Big Joe showed on the field and in the hallways.

The Father looked at Peter and said, "I have created these young people to be four powerhouses of faith. They trust me now with their whole hearts. Their football coach is going to instill in Herman and Joe a winning attitude that will follow them the rest of their lives. Pete, just watch what I do with the four of them. Lucretia and Herman will have a tough time when this is all over with them, but they both know what I have them doing now is going to ensure their being used forever. Joe and Alli are going to be a power couple for life. Watch what I do with them over the next two years and beyond."

It was June 1st. Herman woke up at 10:00 a.m. when his mom started yelling from the bottom of the stairs. "Herman, get your butt out of bed. There is someone here to see you!"

"Good morning, Herm!" Lucretia said sweetly. "Did you forget we have a planning meeting this morning for the Luther League canoe trip? Frank Paulson sent me to get you."

"Canoe trip? What canoe trip?" Herm asked.

With a smile Lucretia replied, "The one you suggested one cold Sunday in January. Remember, you're Herman Mcbrien. When you say something should happen, people make sure it happens. Tell you what. I will share a canoe with you."

Herman looked at his mom for some excuse to not go on the trip. "Look, young man, you started this thing. It may have been an offhand statement that got the ball rolling, but you got the ball rolling. You need to see it through. Lucretia, tell Frank that Herman will be there as soon as possible." Jill said in a firm, motherly voice.

Lucretia nodded and walked out to her car and headed back to Elim Lutheran church to pass on Jill's message to Frank. Herman hit the shower and followed twenty-five minutes later.

The Father looked at Peter. "Pete, I am about to put into Frank's heart how he can use my young servant Herman to touch the youngest kids in the youth group. Remember how I had Eli and Sam put together Bible Baseball? They used that as an ice breaker between the Catholic and Protestant kids. You're about to see a pick-up softball game get out of hand. You're about to see what happens when one young man who does not know me takes my name in vain. I will have that become a learning experience that the young man will never forget. I am about to do something much more dramatic to show these young guys just how potent I can make a young man who is willing to serve me.

The executive board spent hours planning for the canoe trip, right down to all the food they would need and the number of canoes. Finally, they were done. At 7:00 p.m., Bethesda Lutheran from Carlton was coming to play softball against Elim. As it was slow pitch, Alan Paulson would be pitching, and Herman would be playing short stop. He would also be batting third in the line-up. Carlton, being the visiting team, would be up first.

The first batter Scott Smith. He hit a line drive to second. Kenny Swanson snagged it and tossed it to Ed Johnson at first. Second up was Mike Anderson. Andy, as his teammates called him, hit a nice line drive and got on first. Batting third was Gene St. Marie who got on first on a walk. Next up was Jake. He was a tough guy who like to pick fights. He knew Herman as a goodie two shoes from school. He really wanted to pick a fight with him, but try as he might, he could not get Herman to defend himself. He could even slap his face and not get him to strike back.

Jake looked at Allen. Allen threw the pitch. Jake hit a grounder right at Herman. Herm grabbed it with his bare hand and threw it to first. It was a split second late and Jake was safe. Bases were now loaded.

Mark Johnson was now up to bat. He had played baseball with Herm in the spring at Carlton. Herman knew what to expect. Mark hit the ball hard but liked to keep it just above the infielder's heads, dropping it into shallow left field. Herman knew what he was going to do. He took a few steps back just as Mark swung. The ball dropped, and he made a dash to grab it. St. Marie made it to third and headed for home. Jake rounded second, but at the same time he left second, Herman got into the baseline. Jake did not try to stop. He tried to run over Herman, knocking the ball out of his hand. Herman made the tag but was leveled by Jake.

Jake stood over Herman fuming. John Smith the umpire called him out. Jake looked down on Herman and growled through his teeth. "Listen, Mother, stay down or I will beat the -- out of you.

Herman got up. He was confident that what Corrine had taught him would work quite well in this situation. "Jake, if I were you I would re-think that. Don't do something you will regret. "

Big Joe walked up to Jake. "He would have you out in about ten seconds. Why don't you just settle down and get to know Herman? He is a great guy"

With a look of anger and defeat Jake turned and walked back to his teammates. His coach, Tom Younger, walked up to him and said, "Jake, one more of those and you will be off the team. Watch it. Talk to Herman. There something about him that could save you."

"*Save me, I don't need saving. There is no one tougher than I am. I rule by intimidation. I rule this school by having everyone scared of me. I am JAKETOR the great.*" he thought to himself.

The Father looked at Peter. "I love Jake. The life he has at home is not one that will help him grow into the man I want him to be. What comes across as pride and arrogance is fear. It's fear of opening to anyone and sharing who he really is. He is looking for what I am offering. The problem is he is looking in all the wrong places. If he would only put down his defenses, he might just be able to get the help that he needs. I am going to use Herman to reach him, but I will not force the issue. I use everything short of coercion to bring people to myself. He must make the choice."

After their big win against Bethesda, Herman and Joe were walking off the field. Herman looked at Joe and said, "This fall we will all be on the same team. I am going to pull Jake aside and see if I can reach him."

Joe got a serious look on his face. "I don't think there is anyone around who can reach Jake. I would not even bother."

"In II Peter 3:9, Peter wrote that God is slow to anger, not wanting anyone to perish. I must take a chance. I really feel God's leading in trying to get to Jake. I am the servant. If he can be reached, God through Jesus will show me how." Herm replied.

The rest of the summer passed so quickly it seemed like a flash. It was early August and two a-days were approaching already. Not a favorite time of the year for Herman, but he knew that the new play that Coach Erickson had given him in the spring would be an awesome thing.

# The Play

THEIR JUNIOR SEASON OPENED AGAINST Wrenshall. This team always finished last in the Polar League. The game went as anticipated. Herman wanted to run the play. He walked up to Coach Erickson while the team was on defense. Coach Erickson took one look at Herm and knew what he was going to ask. "No!" was his firm answer. Herman shrugged and walked back to his teammates.

"He was pretty clear about what we would not be calling tonight. There is no way we get to run it. I think he is saving it for something special." Herman stated.

At practice they ran the play repeatedly. Big Joe would hit Herm right on the numbers every time. They would play Cromwell, McGregor, and Flood wood with no call for the play. Then came Barnum. Against Barnum they were leading by only one touchdown. Coach Erickson called Joe and Herman over. "Could you guys make it work?" Herman and Joe looked at each other.

"We could, and we will." they said in unison.

Just then, Thompson a young cornerback intercepted a pass from Myhre, the Barnum quarterback, and returned it for a touchdown. At that point, Coach Erickson knew that game was out of reach for Barnum. He looked at the two players who were itching to use the play. "Sorry, boys, we really don't need it tonight. Let's keep that saved for Moose Lake or Esko."

The three players who were to execute the play looked at each other and shook their heads. Big Joe had been wanting to impress Alli with a touchdown pass to Herman for a long time. It seemed that the opportunity would never happen. Their frustration was gaining momentum. They seemed to practice that play every single day. Yet, they questioned if they would ever get to do it. That night they defeated Barnum by a score of 24 to 6.

The Father looked at Jesus and Peter. "Gentlemen, you're about to see me work through my Spirit to teach Joe and Herman a valuable lesson. You see, I will work for decades for a result that I want. I give natural and spiritual gifts to people. I produce fruit. These young men are learning what it means to work in my timing. What these boys don't understand is that when the time is right, things happen. There is a time for that play. If they execute it the way it was designed, it will blow the game wide open."

The regular season came down to the final two games against Moose Lake and Esko. Both teams were perennial powerhouses. Both had a history of ending any hopes Carlton had for winning the Polar League. Year after year, Coach Erickson would come close and then lose big time to both teams. This year could finally be the year to win it all. He drove his players harder and harder. He felt he had to instill in each of them that the pain they felt now would get them through the last two minutes of the most important game. He also knew that if they could push through the pain now, they would be able to endure difficulties off the field as well. They would not quit. They would push themselves to accomplish greatness in whatever they set themselves to do in life. He also knew he had the team working on a play over and over again for a one-time use. He would pull the pin on the grenade of the triple reverse that would make Joe a hero. And he knew Friday night was coming as he smiled to himself slightly.

The second to the last game of the year was upon them. They were at Moose Lake's field. They knew it was going to be a tough game. Carlton's three senior captains walked out to mid field. They shook hands with the two captains of Moose Lake. Carlton lost the toss and elected the wind in their faces, knowing this would give them better options in the second half of the game.

The defense that Coach Erickson implemented stuffed the Lakers with a three and out on their first possession.

The Bulldogs took the field. In the huddle, Herman looked over at Bruce Johnson the freshman fullback who had been burning up the field. "45 power sweep right. Johnson you are lead blocker for Smith on this one. Don't miss it."

The Bulldogs broke the huddle. Herman bent down over the center and called the signals. He took the snap and tossed the ball to Smith flying toward the right end. Johnson, the lead block, crushed the defensive end giving Smith a wide-open field. He ran for 65 yards down to the 3-yard line before he could be stopped.

Herman walked into the huddle. "Let's have some fun with this one. He looked at Big Joe. "Joe, if we run the quarterback draw to your side, can you take out that #54 linebacker before he gets to the line?"

"Call it!" was Joe's quick reply.

They broke the huddle and ran to the line of scrimmage. The ball was snapped. Herman took two steps back. The line backers dropped off and Herman ran to the 2 holes on the left side of the line. #54 spotted what was going on and ran to fill the hole. He was crushed by Big Joe. Herman scampered in for the touchdown. With the extra point that gave them a 14 to 0 lead that expanded to a 32-3 score going into the $4^{th}$ quarter.

Herman walked up to Coach Erickson. The coach knew what he was going to ask. He smiled and shook his head to indicate no.

The Father looked at Peter and smiled. "These young men have one play that will make their career. It will get them into Notre Dame. They will both have full ride scholarships. It will be used only once in their high school careers, and it won't be against Esko."

Peter got a look of bewilderment on his face. "That's the last game of the season. If not, then when?" he asked.

The Father grinned, "Pete, don't forget the playoffs."

The last game of the season was against the Esko Eskimos. Carlton and Esko had been archrivals for years. Years and years ago six members of the 1973 junior class of Carlton melted the Igloo of the Eskimos, and the Eskimos had not forgotten. Their rivalry was the stuff of legends. Herman and Big Joe were anxious to open the game with THE play, but they would soon find out it was not to be.

Coach Erickson knew that if he won this game, he would have his first trip to the state tournament. He did not mention it to the team because he did not want to put undue pressure on them. The team was already strung tighter than a bass drum. However, despite his caution, it was something they already knew, and they were all contemplating the possibility of getting to be in the state tournament.

That Friday night, the stadium was packed. Out-of-town press was also present for this high school football game. Esko was loaded for bear. They were out to demolish the Bulldogs for that long-ago incident with the Igloo. (40 years prior some Bulldog jocks melted the igloo they had spent weeks building.) Coach Erickson was ready to turn their anger into an asset. Esko won the toss and elected to receive the kick-off. Erickson called the offense over and told them, "These guys are ready to pound you. They see you as their archrival. When they go on defense, their ears are going to be tied back, and they are going to be coming across that line in a way you have not seen before. We will make that totally ineffective by simply calling a screen pass on the first play from scrimmage." He looked at Herman, called a 25-screen right, and instructed the line to hold for two seconds and then release.

Esko went three and out against the stubborn Bulldog defense. Herman went into the huddle. "25 screen right. Linemen hold the blocks for two seconds. On two break." The Bulldogs went to the line. Herman bent down under his center. "Go, Go," he called, and the ball was snapped. He knew he had two seconds before the rush happened. Big Joe leveled the tackle across from him, then stepped around to block down field. Herman saw the rush coming and flipped the ball to Smith who was running in the open field. The line men waited for Smith to take the ball in and then they crushed the linebackers and corner backs. Smith was able to outrun the safety and get to the end zone for a touchdown. The crowd went wild. The years of getting used as a mop on a very dirty floor were finally over, at least for now. For the first time in years Jim Erickson had a complete team. Carlton went on to win the game 24 to 6. The defense did not allow a touchdown. Carlton had won the Polar League, and the state playoffs started the next Friday.

"Pete, what you are about to see next is rewards for some people. The first one, is to Coach Erickson. He has been a faithful servant of mine for years. For years, decades even, he has taught young men the value of teamwork and good sportsmanship. He has honored me in everything he has done. His reward is seeing the young boys I have put before him become great men. Some have become great followers of me. The second one is going to Herman. His reward is going to go on for years, but right now it will one of taking his team to the greatest heights that Carlton has ever known. I give gifts. When those gifts are used for my glory, and a person works hard to achieve the greatness I have instilled in them, they will see success. Those rewards can be admiration from vast numbers of people or just the quiet feeling knowing they have change others' lives forever."

Herman walked into school on Monday. The regular season was over. He walked up to Big Joe. "Joe, what do you think? Will we ever run that play?"

Joe smiled. "I would love to throw one touchdown pass in my career."

Herman smiled. "I'm sure impressing Alli has nothing to do with it, bro!"

Just then Coach Erickson walked up to the two boys. "Gentlemen, you have someone in the office who want to talk to you. Be careful what you say."

Coach Erickson escorted the boys into the office. Standing there was a reporter from the Duluth News Gazette along with reporters from all the television stations in the area. They all proceeded into the board room, so the reporters could ask their questions. The first reporter asked, "Herman, to what do you credit with your absolute success?"

Herman stood in silence for just a moment. He looked at Coach Erickson smiled and said, "There are several things that went into this winning season that we were so blessed to have. I want to give credit to where credit is due. Without the absolute team work that happened on this team this year, we couldn't win. First, I want to thank my Heavenly Father. He arranged everything. He had things happened that brought me here for such a time as this. I am blessed to have a team around me that works like a well-oiled machine. God arranged these guys to be at Carlton High School. He arranged it for Coach Erickson to have the best group of talent he has ever had. He then showed Coach Erickson to drive us to success. Thank you." Herman sat down.

Big Joe was the next one to take questions. The reporter, hoping to get a juicy point, asked, "So tell us, Joe, do you have any secret plays for the play offs?"

Joe got a panicked look on his face, looked at Coach Erickson for help. Coach Erickson smiled and shook his head no. "Look, you guys, if we did and I told you, then it would not be a secret." he said smiling.

"How about the name of one?" the reporter asked.

Joe thought to himself. "*We have no name it. So, I can say.*" "Nope, I cannot give you a name I don't have." Joe answered with a confident smile.

With that Coach Erickson said, "Thank you." and sent the boys back to class.

The Father looked at Thumbnail and said. "Little buddy, you listen well. When I had you tell the coach to end it, you were able to have the coach avoid the next question. That question was 'So, do you have a play that you have not named yet?' That would have placed my servant Joe in a position of having to lie. You did well little one."

Thumbnail became excited. "Father, nothing makes me happier than to hear well done from you. These young men are going to be most exciting to watch over the next few years."

At practice that night Coach Erickson had a little surprise for his team. "Tonight, gentleman, we name the play. We have practiced it all season. We will continue to practice it. I know that I am not supposed to talk about God or Jesus in a public school, but I feel compelled to tell you that we are all given God-given talents. You gentlemen have worked with the talents you have been given for this game all year. Yet one never reaches the ultimate in their gifts. You can become better and better with whatever gifts you have been given, but mastery is something that cannot be achieved.

The name of the play is going to be one word. Payday. This play will be used once in the playoffs. It will be used to defeat the one team that can stop us from achieving the ultimate victory. It will be used for the most crucial victory in your high school career. We don't know if we will ever get back here, but if you do what I tell you, and play to the full extent of your capabilities, you will be champions. Let's go to work."

The focus of the team that week was amazing to behold. They all knew what was at stake. They all remembered those two a-days in August. They all remembered what it was like to sweat and hurt after each practice. They knew for some of them, the seniors, this was their last chance. Granted some of them would go onto college ball, but for most them, this would be it. This would be their one shot to win a championship, and that memory would last a lifetime. They would not let this moment pass them by.

The Father of all mankind looked at Peter and Jesus. "Gentlemen, what you're about to see is what happens when a team listens to the prompting of my spirit for an extended period of time. You're about to see what happens when I have a coach who knows my voice and has been a loyal and devoted servant of mine for years. I always get the victory, even out of defeat on the field, I win." Pete looked at the Father and asked, "Father, are we going to see defeat here? Is that where you are going to get the victory?"

The Father got a look of compassion then chuckled a bit, "Pete, you know that I never give away the "play" before it's called. Just watch, and you will see some awesome football. Then you are going to see my glory in ways you have seldom seen it before. You know I like to surprise people in big ways. The championship game is going to be something people talk about for years and years to come."

The next three weeks of practice were vicious, but the team kept thinking how victory would be so sweet. Finally, the title game, played at the new Minnesota Vikings stadium was upon them. It would be a game for the ages. They were playing Milaca in the state final. Milaca had a reputation as a no-nonsense team that was brutal from the kickoff to the final gun. They had sent more players from opponents' teams to the hospital during the regular than any team in the history of the game. They expected to do no less to the Carlton Bulldogs.

During the last week of practice, Coach Erickson knew what Milaca's ruthless coach would have in mind, so he spent the week preparing his team for the onslaught that was about to come their way. After practice on the Friday before the big game, they all understood what they were up against. Coach Erickson had spent some time after practice in the locker room telling them what to expect. When he finished talking about the tactics of the team they would be facing, he told them the story of David and Goliath.

He walked into the locker room. "Gentlemen, tomorrow we face a team that is big and tough. They don't know the meaning of the word sportsmanship. We are going to teach them. Now, you all know the Supreme Court says I can't make you pray. However, if one of you guys want to lead a prayer I won't stop you."

Herman stepped forward. "Father in heaven, time after time your children came against strong odds and you gave them the victory. Saul got into trouble when you gave him a victory, but he did not conquer the way you told him to. Father, normally I would not ask for a victory, but this team we are facing is led by a coach who has his players physically hurt other teams, so they can get the victory. David, when he came against Goliath, had one simple prayer before he slew that big, bad guy. 'Not by might, nor by power, but by my spirit, says the Lord.' Father, we give this game to you. We ask that you get the glory out of it. That if we get the win that we give you the credit. No, Lord, let me rephrase that. When we win, make sure we give you the credit." He then led the rest of the players in the Lord's Prayer, and with the final Amen, they loaded the bus and went back to the hotel.

The emotions of the players were tense. They all were talking and pacing back and forth in their rooms. All except one. Joe looked at his roommate Herman. "Herm, how in the world can you be so cool about this whole thing? Tomorrow is the biggest game of our lives. Aren't you anxious?"

Herman looked across the room at Big Joe. "Look, it's like this, tomorrow we walk out into that stadium. We are going to use everything at our disposal to win this game. Knowing the reputation of their coach, I would guess that he is not a praying man. God the Father will not be mocked. He sent Jesus the Christ to save us from our sin, but he also sent his Holy Spirit to lead us into all things. He sent us one of the greatest high school coaches of all time. We have a coach who is more interested in making us great men than he is his own winning record. This year, Our Father in Heaven through His Son by His Holy Spirit has given Coach Erickson his dream team. He has given Coach Erickson "Payday." Joe, I will guarantee you this, when the time is right the coach will call the play. It will be a success. You will throw me a perfect pass, and I will score. This game will be a fight to end all high school football game fights, but before this game, this team will hear what my dad yelled only once in his whole baseball career. You will hear it the first time I come to the line. As God is my witness, if we play the game God is calling us to, we will win tomorrow."

The Father had a huge smile on his face as he looked at his Son Jesus the Christ. "Son, Eli is about to experience the greatest thrill a father can have. That second you walked out of the grave I felt it. The total rush of emotion when you see your son totally succeed at what he was meant to do. When you walked out of the grave, my pride for you filled the universe. My Spirit could now indwell mankind's heart. If these boys don't leave anything on the field, then Eli will experience that joy."

Jesus the Christ looked at his Father, smiled, and said," Thanks, Dad."

The next morning the phone in Herman's room rang. "Herman, here." he answered.

"Herm, this is your dad. Just thought your mom and I would call to tell you just how proud we are of you. I remember my first championship in high school. It was a rush. But, Son, don't forget to have fun. We have been praying for you, and we will be all day."

"Thanks, Dad. That means a lot to me. God is in control of the whole thing. We will win this game if we all play to our potential. We cannot hide the talent we have been given. We have to use that talent to the maximum of our ability. We cannot back down. We must give everything to the Lord on every play. When I complete a pass, or I hand the ball off to a back and he runs for a huge gain, the credit goes to our Father in heaven. On every play, we are all sacrificing to the Lord of Heaven and Earth. On every play, we are giving back to God our Father through His Son by His Holy Spirit a bit of the talent he has given us. Dad, we have one shot at this. We don't know if we will ever be in the game again. Every play has to be played with one reason behind it – to give it back to God our Father for his glory."

The day dragged by. It seemed like the time to play would never come, but it did. Coach Erickson walked into the locker room and looked at his team chomping at the bit to get ready. "Gentlemen, we are now at the end of the road. We will either come away with the state title or we won't. My question to you is how badly do you want it?

Twenty-five years from now, when you look at your first grandchild, will you be able to tell that child that you left everything on the field, or will you have regret that you did not give it everything you had? This team is mean, and they are dirty. They hurt a lot of people and they don't care. They are Goliath. How bad do you want it?"

Just then Dennis Wolf walked in. He had graduated the spring of the preceding year. "Hey, guys! Just thought I would stop by and wish you well. Leave nothing on the field. Your opponent has one thing on their mind – seeing how many of you they can hurt. It's up to you to take that out of them early. They have never faced a squad that is as sportsmanship minded as you are. I just feel like I am supposed to tell you this. Meet force with force. Don't back down, whatever they give you, give it back double. Go with Jesus and win this game!" With that Wolf turned and walked out into the stands of the dome.

The team walked to the opening of the tunnel that led to the field. Herman looked around the stadium. Fifty thousand football fans from all over the state of Minnesota were there to watch the final four games for the division A to AAAA championships. Carlton versus Milaca would be a game that would be talked about for years. Two little schools with teams that were tough and unyielding against all their opponents. One team would play and win using tactics that honored the Great I Am of the universe. The other could be likened to Jesus 'words in the Gospel of John: "The thief comes to kill, steal, and destroy." The problem Milica would face this night was that the Carlton Bulldogs would play the game like Pitbulls. They would not let go of that which God created them to do.

Through four quarters the teams battled to a 7 to7 tie. Every time Milaca would try to get a late hit and try to hurt Herman, Big Joe would crush the person trying to do the damage. They had to carry two of the players, sent by their coach to take care of Herman, off the field.

The seconds were ticking away. It was down to the last twenty-five seconds, time for one last play. Herman called a time out and trotted to the sideline to meet with Coach Erickson. Coach Erickson looked at Herman and said, "Payday.!"

Herman trotted back to the huddle. He looked at his teammates. He looked at Big Joe and said with a grin, "Joe, it's time to end this thing." He called the play. "Payday on 2. Let's go!"

The center called, "Break" and the team went to the line.

The center, Johnson, went down over the ball.

Herman called the signals. "Down, Set, Go! Go!" Johnson snapped the ball.

Herman stepped back and handed the ball to Derusha the running back. Derusha then started to run to his right. He handed the ball to Big Joe, pulling from his left tackle to the right. Herman was streaking down the right sideline. Joe saw him and laid the ball out perfectly for a touchdown. Herman ran into the end zone and the crowd went absolutely insane. Carlton won their first and only State Championship.

As they walked into the locker room, the team was beyond excited. Their emotions were flying high. Yet the trip home was one of somber quietness. The team knew that what they had as a team that year was over. They all knew that they would never again play at that level as a high school team. They knew that many of them would never play together again. This mood conflicted with the joy of the moment.

Coach Erickson had expected a party atmosphere on the way home. As he walked onto the bus, he immediately noticed how quite it was. One would think the team had lost. There was a solemnity on the bus that no one had anticipated, and there was something in it that the coach knew he had to get to the bottom of.

Peter looked at the Father. "Father, what's going on here. These guys should be over the top with joy. I just saw them on the field with an excitement that very few teams ever get to experience. What's going on here?

The Father looked over at Peter and said, "Pete, these boys have worked their behinds off all season. They had a goal, and they reached it. Now they are discovering something quite normal. To gain the world and the best the world has to offer is an empty thing. Unless there is a plan for using a victory for my glory, the victory becomes empty. Remember what I had my servant Solomon write: 'Vanities, vanities, all is but vanity.' Without me in the center of anything, even the biggest victory becomes an empty thing. Coach Erickson is about to give these young men a lesson that will draw them to me."

"Okay, men, we need to talk. You have worked harder than any team I have ever coached. You won a victory at the beginning of the season no one thought you would win. As we sit here on this bus, I have a feeling you're all asking yourselves, now what? It's over, now what?" Coach Erickson continued, "It's like this. Your lives are just starting. You now know what sacrifice is all about. What I am about to share with you could cost me my job, but I ask myself one question, what would Jesus do?" He paused and then continued, "There was a baby born over 2000 years ago. He grew into a man with a goal set before him. This goal would not be an easy one to complete, but when it was completed, the victory would be won, not for a single season, but forever.

Your victory tonight was the end of a long season. The ultimate victory that you won was the end of a game, a season, and for you seniors your high school football career. Yet you will take what it took to get to that victory with you forever. The victory you won tonight was a 48-minute game. At the end of it you were victors, yet there is an emptiness. What now? What now? Gentlemen, there are two courses for your life. God the Father has one, and the enemy of your souls also has one. The question each and every one of us has to ask is this: who do we choose to serve? One gave his life and walked out of the grave to give us the victory. The other wants to destroy us and make us his slaves for eternity in a lake of fire. Who do you want to serve? I can't pray with you. But you do have some teammates who will. I won't identify them; you know who they are." With that, Coach Erickson turned and sat down.

The Father looked at Peter with a seriousness he had not seen recently. "Pete, watch now. I am about to have Herman and Big Joe pray with most of the young men on this team. Carlton High school will be mine."

Pete simply nodded. He could hardly wait to see what the Father had in mind.

The bus ride back to the hotel was a short one. The thirty-five tired yet excited football players, for the first time in four months, could now relax. The final victory was theirs. Yet for the seniors on the team, this was it. This was the final game for all but one senior who would go on to play college ball. This amazing victory gave them a happy memory that would last a lifetime. Many of the team's seniors took the opportunity to pray with their Junior star quarterback Herman and his best friend Big Joe to have Jesus the Christ enter their hearts and start the journey that would lead many of them to greatness in other fields.

During the remainder of the next two years, Carlton athletics shone. They were league champs in football, basketball, and baseball. Many of the players came to Christ, as God the Father by His Son the Christ through His Holy Spirit touched the players that Herman interacted with.

The Last Week at Carlton

The Father looked at Peter. The somber look on God the Father's face caught Peter somewhat off guard. "Pete, things start, and things end. This week will be one of many things happening. It will be a whirlwind of events. But this is the beginning of the end for several things in all four of their lives. All four of these kids have an amazing future ahead of them. Herman and Joe's will be intertwined. Alli and Lu will also have great futures. I lead people in the ways I need them to go. Remember what I said about Eli that I could tell when a person is young whether they were going to serve me or not? Eli was going to serve me. He did, and he does to this day."

"Father does that mean that there are no permanent relationships here?"

"Pete, there are four permanent relationships here, but you have to stay tuned to see what they are going to look like. Remember this. I really do have everything under control. Just stay tuned."

Carlton had changed. There had been a new spirit in the building for four years. It was the Holy Spirit that had been working for years through Herman, Big Joe, Lucretia, and Alli. They all knew that this summer would be the last they would all be together, but their friendship would continue for the rest of their lives.

At lunch that Monday, Lu was sitting with Herman. She smiled at him and asked, "Do you remember that day we swam out to the raft at Sandy Lake?"

"Do I ever! As I lay there on the raft and looked at you standing over me in that bikini it was tough to get my mind where it needed to be. It was as if this little voice in my ear to stand up and talk to you about going and getting something else on.

Thumbnail, in the Father's presence, smiled knowing it was he who had been speaking into the ear of Herman.

"Herman that day changed my life. It changed my attitude towards relationships. It made me realize that a friendship is more important than a physical relationship. I know now what God's choice is for a relationship."

Herman looked over at Lu and smiled. "Lu, I was tempted to try to take it in a direction that it should not have gone, but as we honor our Father in Heaven he will honor us."

The bell sounded ending lunch. They all headed to class.

"Peter, this summer is going to be two things for Lu and Herman. It will be magical, and it will be tough as nails."

"What do you mean Father?" Pete responded.

"Pete, it's like this. The chemistry between them is going to be intense. Yet they will not allow it to control them because of their caring for Me and each other. They both know they will have to be apart for their college years. They both know without a doubt at the end of this summer they will only see each other at their 10-year reunion. However, this summer will be magical, and those memories will last them a lifetime.

The morning after graduation Herman was sleeping very, very soundly. His phone had rung three times already, but it was on the table in the dining room. The next time it rang, Jill grabbed it and headed upstairs. She threw open the door to Herman's room, pulled off the covers, handed him his phone and said. "Hey, Buster, every five minutes this phone has interrupted our conversations. It's time for you to get your behind out of that bed and call Lu back. I have a feeling she wants to do something with you today."

Herman took his phone from his mother's hand. He looked at the phone and saw he had missed several calls from Lu. He hit the redial button and promptly heard Lu's phone ring. He heard on the other end, "Good morning, Champ. It's our last summer together. How about taking your best friend on a long motorcycle ride to celebrate!?"

Herman smiled to himself. "How could I turn down one of the prettiest girls ever to graduate from Carlton High School? Let me hit the shower, and I will be at your doorstep in an hour." He hung up the phone and headed for the shower.

As he came bounding down the stairs Jill was waiting at the bottom for him. "What's on your agenda today, Mister?"

"We are gonna hop on the Honda and go for a long ride to celebrate graduation. Who knows where we are going to end up."

Jill got a sly grin on her face. "Remember that promise that my dad got your father to agree to? How about you make that promise to me?"

"Mom, I love you a bunch. But as I think about it, for whatever reason God has, I cannot make that promise. I don't know why but I can't. We both know that romantically we both feel it. We both also know that God does not have us for each other in the long run. We both know that to have a successful marriage one must be able to trust one's partner. We cannot risk future relationships by allowing our physical attraction to each other to get the better of us. God has plans for us in his purpose. We both know that those plans don't include us together. We will always be close friends. Hopefully, our future spouses will be okay with our friendship and we can all do fun things together. If not, we can accept that. This is our summer. We are going to just have a good time with the time God gives us this summer. Mom, you have to just trust me on this one."

Jill looked at her son with a pride that could burst her buttons. She knew he had his Father in heaven as well has the character of his dad Eli in him. She trusted him, so she smiled and kissed him on the cheek. "Have fun, be good!"

The summer went by in a blur. The happy memories Herman and Lu created would be held by them for the rest of their lives. They did not compromise their principles of purity, and they had a fun summer of softball, swimming, and companionship with their friends and classmates.

Finally, it was Mid-August. The Carlton County Fair was happening in Barnum. Herman and Lu hopped on Herman's Honda and rode down for the day. They spent hours walking around the fairgrounds. As the evening rolled around, and the lights of the fair came on and twinkled in the dusk, Herman and Lu walked through the shadows, occasionally looking into each other's eyes. Thoughts of *what if?* ran through both of their minds, but then they would both put the thoughts out of their minds again.

As the lights of the fair started to go out for the year, they walked to where the bike was parked. The both put on their helmets and got on the bike. They paused just before straddling the seat. They looked at each other and smiled. Without a word they climbed on the bike, Herman started it, and they headed for Lu's parents.

As they pulled up the driveway they noticed the light on over the doorway. They walked up to it. Herman said although he already knew, "Next year you are at Gustavus, right?"

With a tear running down her cheek, Lu looked at Herman. She didn't want to say goodbye. Her emotions and desire to stay with Herman felt overwhelming, but both Herman and Lu knew that what they felt could never be acted on. "That's correct. I will be a Gustie Lion next year." she said, forcing a smile.

"Lu, I will remember this summer forever. You and I both know that our Father in heaven has a different path for each of us in his purpose." He took her by the hand and walked her to the door. They looked into each other's eyes. The feelings between them were powerful. Herman put his index finger under Lu's chin, raised it, and kissed her lips ever so lightly. With tears flowing, he stepped back slightly. "We both know that was the only kiss we will ever have. Just know this. In Jesus' name, I love you. That love is pure and holy. That will never change. But our roles in our Father's kingdom have to be greater than the emotions we feel now."

Lu was crying from deep within her being. She was feeling such a loss, yet she knew in her heart they were making the right decision. "Herman, in Jesus' name, I love you too." She got on her toes and kissed his cheek. "Herman you were and are my first real love. You have shown me how a true man treats a lady. I don't know where these lives we have been given will take us. But know this, Mister. I want to be used to see lives changed. I really do love you, but I also know that the sacrifice that Christ made on the Cross, and his victory over the grave, is what we must be about. Herman, I leave for St. Peter tomorrow, you leave for South Bend. I don't know if we will see much of each other ever again. But I do know what the Father has for me. I know what Father has for you. I promise to never quit praying for you. Please pray for me.

We have so much to accomplish. If our paths cross again I will be blessed."

Herman looked at Lu and smiled. He started to say something, but Lu put her fingers to his lips, and went inside. The tears started to run like a river down Herman's cheeks. He turned and walked back to his bike. He sat there for a couple minutes to regain his composure before trying to ride home. He wondered when and if he would ever see this amazing girl again. He just did not know. But he would treasure his memories of her forever.

"Pete; what these two are going to learn is that I put people together for a reason. Sometimes that reason is for protection of one or both individuals. Sometimes it's for protection of them, but also to be used as an outreach to others, so the others can be drawn to me. A person's youth is an exciting time for them. Everything is new. When a youth is guided by my spirit, it can become especially exciting for them. I put Herman and Lu together for a season. They learned from each other what my grace and love look like. They honored me in their relationship. I have something new for both in college. I am going to use them in different venues to draw thousands to me. It's going to be exciting to watch.

"Father, I have this incredible urge to ask you what you have planned. But I already know the answer. Stay tuned, lol"

"Pete! You understand! After all these centuries you understand!" the Father said with a hearty chuckle.

# New Beginnings.

It was mid-August and the first day of two- a-days at the University of Notre Dame. Herman walked into the locker room not knowing what to expect. During the recruitment phase, he had met with Coach Johnson. He understood the winning ways of the Fighting Irish. He knew that what would be expected of him was only 150% on every play. He also knew as a freshman, he would not walk out and be a star like in high school; he would have to earn it. He sat on the bench in the locker room quietly praying for the guidance he would need over the next few years. As he sat there, Coach Johnson walked up behind him. He placed a hand on Herman's shoulder. "Herman, the adventure your about to embark on is glorifying God our Father. This university, as you well know, is a Catholic university, and above all else we will glorify the Father in all we do here. We will win football games. But what we do has to be a platform for the players to learn how to go beyond themselves to win at whatever they do with the rest of their lives. Herman, I will push you beyond where you have ever been physically. Do you have the mental toughness to handle it? If you do, in the end, you will be a champion."

The Father looked at Peter. "Pete, now the rubber hits the road. Eli worked his behind off to accomplish greatness in baseball. Herman is about to get himself pounded into the ground and dig himself out to accomplish my greatness. He is going to accomplish a greatness he did not know he was capable of. This is going to be fun to watch."

Herman was sleeping in the dorm at Notre Dame. Out in the hallway he heard the coaches yelling at the top of their lungs. "Let's go, rookies, the time for slumber is over. You don't have your mommies to cook and make your breakfast. All those headlines are gone. You gotta get out of those nice warm beds and hit the cold Indiana mornings now. You're in the big time now. Let's get those lazy butts out of bed and onto that field!"

Herman crawled out of the bunk. He hated morning almost as much as his dad Eli did. But this morning he knew he had something to prove. He soon found out, however, that he would not even touch a football for the first two days. He would not hand it off or throw a pass. The first two days were to find out who really had what it took to play big time Division I football.

The coaches expected him to wash out. They seemed to forget two things. One, he was a child of the Highest God, who had been bought by the very blood that Jesus Christ had shed on the cross. And two, he was the son of the great Eli Mcbrien. He had greatness built into his genes. He would not quit but become better and better the harder they worked him.

After the third day of practice, Herman walked into his dorm room, dropped on his bunk, put his hands over his head, and thought to himself. "*This is brutal. Never in my wildest dreams did I ever think I would be worked this hard. Becoming part of the Fighting Irish is either going to kill me or make me indestructible.*" It was at that point that Jeff Hanks his center walked into his room.

"Hey Mac! A bunch of us guys are meeting with the Intervarsity chapter on campus to start getting things put together for the fall welcome for incoming freshmen. They thought they would try to recruit a bunch of believing football players to help. You in?"

Herman went to jump out of his bunk to go to work and help the chapter. He moved and experienced pain like he had not felt before. "Man, I am so sore. I have never worked like this before." He said crawling out of his bunk, so he could help.

Jeff looked at Herman and chuckled. "Mac, one thing you will learn for next year. Spend the summer working out.

Stay in shape all winter and spring. If you don't next year will be worse than this one."

Herman and Jeff walked across campus to meet with the gang from Intervarsity Christian Fellowship. They walked into the gym where the gala was being set up for the incoming freshman. Abby a cute little blonde walked up to Jeff and Herman and smiled. "Jeff, where did you find this great looking guy?"

Jeff smiled. "This is Mac."

Before he could say anymore Herman interjected. "Hi, my name is Herman Mcbrien. I am the new freshman quarterback."

Jeff chuckled. "This is Mac. He will be a star if he will ever loosen up and enjoy life here on campus."

Abby walked up to Herman and took his hand in hers. "Mac, eh! Well, Mr. Mac, I am just going to have to get to know you a bit." Abby said as she smiled broadly at Herman.

Herman realized that he was speechless. He could not think of a thing to say. Every time he would open his mouth to say something he stammered. He finally was able to get a few words out. "What do you need me to do?" he said as he smiled at Abby.

Abby looked at him and said, "Follow me." For the next few hours she used his 6'2" frame to reach high stuff she could not. When the work was done, she looked at Herman and smiled. "Mac! Would you join me at the mixer tomorrow night? I think I would really like to get to know you."

He smiled and thought to himself. *"I am going to get Jeff for sticking me with that handle Mac. That handle will probably be mine for the rest of my college career, not to mention if I make it to the pro's. I will get him. Yes, sir I will."* "Abby, I am flattered, and I would love to come as your friend, but I will not be staying long. I have to have every play and every assignment of every player down before the first game of the season. When I am on the sideline and the coach gives me a play it must open like data on a computer. I have to have it quicker than the fastest computer. I must know which player does what. Each player must know his plays. The quarterback has to know everything."

Abby smiled. "I understand. You have to be a know it all." she said, laughing.

"Abby, you're a sweet girl. But I gotta be upfront. I really don't want anything other than friendships. Our Father in Heaven has a call on me. Other than football I don't know for sure what it is, or what it's going to look like. I do know it's gonna be good." As he walked away he shook his head and thought. "*Father protect this lovely work of art you have created. There are a lot of guys out there who would love to take advantage of this young lady. I know if I were to give into such desires, and I would like to, it could wreck a lot of plans you have made. I know we are created for so much more. If you have a bride for me, you will show her to me. I just pray your protection on Abby!*"

Thumbnail looked to the Father for some direction. The Father smiled. "Thumbnail, Herman will have a role in her growth, both as a person and as a believer in me, but they're not going to become a couple. They are my kids who will serve me forever. Just not together beyond college."

The Father smiled as he told Peter, "See what Eli has instilled in Herman? He has instilled my values. Young men are to protect the young ladies I bring across their path, not take advantage of them. Sometimes when the attraction is strong, it's tough for young men to do what I have created them to accomplish. But the ones who really love me will do the right thing and doing the right thing will bring them true greatness."

Peter looked at the Father and smiled as he said, "Herman has learned from his father well, but did not his mom have something to do with his greatness also?"

"Pete, Herman learned a great many very valuable things from his mother. However, the ability to honor a young lady whether she is going to be someone special to him or a friend is taught by the father. As we look around and see boys treating young ladies like objects to be used and discarded, it is often because that's the way they saw their fathers treat their mothers. All Herman ever saw with Eli and Jill was Eli honoring his wife. When a man honors the gift I have given him, I also honor him." The Father stated this with an authority that threw Peter back a bit. This topic is one the Father cares much about.

The next morning Jeff was pounding on Herman's door. "Mac! Get your butt out of that bed. It's Abby!" he said in a panicked state.

Herman bolted out of his bunk. He smashed his head on the top bunk he jumped up so quickly. "What's going on?"

"Come quick!"

They ran down the hall to Abby's room. When they entered it, they found their friend had been attacked. A male student had snuck into her room and hidden in her closet. "It was Jack Smith. After he hit me, I screamed. My roommate Judy walked in as he threw me on the bed. She saw him, and he ran out."

"What she is saying is true." Judy confirmed.

Jack was on the football team, and both Herman and Jeff knew him well. Herman turned to Jeff. "Let's go. We know what we have to do."

Jeff nodded. Thumbnail landed quickly on Herman's shoulder. "Take this slow, Herman. This sort of thing can get out of control quickly."

Herman walked over to Abby. "Let me call the campus police. He needs to be taught a lesson, and to be made an example of. I was raised to respect women. This guy was raised by a bum."

"Mac, he came onto me. He told me that you could have any girl you wanted. He was going to make sure you would not want me." Abby said in tears.

Herman looked at Abby. "If you only knew. but we both know our Father has something else for both of us. As for Jack, I think we could get his scholarship pulled because of this. Jeff let's go talk to Coach Johnson."

Jeff pulled out his cell phone and called the coach to set up a meeting between Herman, Jeff, and Coach Johnson. Within a short time, they walked into his office and sat down across from their coach. Coach Johnson looked at the two young men sitting across from him. "Look Jeff and Mac, I have heard the stories. I know both of you gentlemen to be men of honor. Are the stories true?"

Jeff and Herman both look at each other. Herman spoke up. "Coach, I ran into Abby's room shortly after Jack left. It would have been a lot worse if her roommate Judy had not walked into the room and saw what Jack was trying to do. He pushed by Judy and ran out."

At that point Jack walked into coach Johnson's office. "These guys and those girls are trying to frame me. "

Coach Johnson noticed the scratch on Jack's cheek. "Where did that scratch come from. It looks fresh. I think I will call the campus police and see about a DNA test."

A look of fear came over Jack's face. "All right. I did it. When I was in high school the girls were all over me. I…"

Coach Johnson with that called Abby into his office. "Abby, If I pull his scholarship and have him off campus by morning, would that be satisfactory for you?"

She looked at Herman and Jeff. "Can we talk outside for a moment?"

The two boys nodded, and they walked outside the coach's office. "Ok, I need some advice. I know I could run him out of school. I could destroy his career, both college and maybe pro. But what would Christ have me do?" She said almost crying. Then she got a twinkle in her eye as she asked. "Has he been open to what the Christian students have been trying to do on campus?"

Both Herman and Jeff shook their heads. "Why don't we give him a sentence that can change his life?" Abby stated with total passion.

They all agreed and walked back into Coach Johnson's office. The three looked at Coach Johnson as Abby spoke. "Here is what we are willing to do. You get active with Intervarsity Christian Fellowship, come to all the Bible studies for the rest of your time here at Notre Dame, and I will not press any charges. You refuse, and you are out of here tomorrow."

Jack looked at them and realized that he was not able to argue. "Thank you for your mercy. You have a deal. "

Coach Johnson looked at Herman and said. "Mac, I am seeing that you really are going to be a leader here. It's going to be a fun four years. You have practice in an hour, go get ready."

Jack looked at Abby as they left the coaches office. "Why did you not hang me out to dry. I cannot believe what you have done for me?

Abby stopped and looked him straight in the eye. "Look, right now you are not one of my favorite people. What you tried to take from me is something I am saving for the one-man God has set aside for me. If you ever, I mean ever, try to force yourself on anyone else, I am going to make sure that my friends here make sure you will never have children you can call your own. On top of that, I will have you in prison. God the Father is about redemption. You had better take advantage of the redemption he is offering." She turned to Herman and Jeff and said, "Mac and Jeff walk me back to my dorm, would you?" As they walked she looked up at Herman, blinked back the tears and said, "Do you think I did the right thing? He should be in jail for what he tried to do to me. I just don't know if I did the right thing."

Jeff looked at her with an empathetic look on his face. "Abby, the only one who really knows the answer to that question is God himself. You have a strong case if you choose to prosecute. I do have a feeling there will be payment for his crime. What do you think Mac?"

Herman smiled. "Let's talk about that after we get this precious child of the King back to her room."

After they dropped Abby off, each giving her a warm hug, they headed back. Jeff turned to Herman and asked. "Mac, just what do you have in mind?"

Herman got a grin on his face. "It's like this Jeff, God the Father held the Virgin Mary in highest esteem. I think we need to take a lesson from what God the Father would have done if anyone had touched Mary. We have a football team made up of gentlemen. None of whom would take kindly to anyone trying to do that to their sister. I think it's time for a little divine retribution."

Peter looked at the Father and the Son and the Holy Spirit. Fear filled Peter's heart as he understood what Herman and Jeff were about to set up at practice that night. "Father are you going to allow what Herman and Jeff are about to do to Jack?"

The Father spoke with the tone of a loving Father. "Peter, Jack needs to be taught a lesson. If his father had not treated his mother with dishonor, he would not be in this place now. I have role for Jack in my purpose. But he will learn a hard lesson tonight at practice. He will be punished, for what he tried to do to my little girl. He will have no permanent bodily damage, but the lesson he is about to learn will like a little boy being spanked for disrespecting his mother. He will learn his lesson and go on from there."

Herman and Jeff walked into practice, looked around and called their teammates over for a meeting. "Gentlemen, we have a problem. One of our teammates tried to force himself on a young lady in her dorm. I shudder to think what would have happened if her roommate had not came running in when the she screamed. She laid out some conditions for him not to be prosecuted. The first was to get involved with Intervarsity Christian Fellowship. Gentlemen, I think there needs to be more done. The culprit is Jack. Should we give him a taste of what is coming his way if this ever happens again?" Herman stated with a total authority.

Coach Johnson walked over to the teammates. "Gentlemen, what do you have going on here?"

"Coach you don't want to know. You will figure it out tonight in practice. Teams discipline their own." Jeff responded.

"Men, I don't want any."

Herman responded. "Coach no one will get hurt."

"Mac, 'Vengeance is mine, I will repay says the Lord.'" Coach Johnson said with a tone of warning.

"Coach, sometimes the Lord uses those closest to us for his discipline. This is one of those times." Herman responded.

At that point Jack walked into the locker room. Everybody on the squad walked over to the other side of the room. Jack got a worried look on his face as deep down inside he had an idea what was about to go down. He suspected that this practice was going to be part of the punishment for his actions earlier that day.

Jeff, a cornerback, had discussed with the rest of the team what was going to happen. Coach Johnson walked in and made an announcement. "Today, we play full contact, offense against defense. Is everyone ok with that?" The whole team knew what was coming and they knew why.

As they walked out to the field the team knew that the only people going full out would be the pass defense and Jack. They knew that this team would discipline its own. Coach Johnson had taught this team when you hit someone make them feel it. Hit hard. Hit clean but hit hard. The first play was a 25 slant. On this play Jack's assignment was to run a pattern slanting over the middle. Herman called the play, and as Jack crossed over the middle, he caught the ball and was immediately hit hard and put flat on his back by Jeff. Jack got up, shook his head and ran back to the huddle. Herman called the play again and again and again. Each time Jeff slammed him to the ground. Everyone on the team knew what was going on, including Jack.

Jack walked back into the huddle. His nose bloody, his ribs hurting, and his strength almost gone. "Mac, I get it."

Herman looked him in the eye. "25 slant." Break.

As Jack ran up to the line he looked to heaven. "I get it, God. Your kids are protected by you. You put it on people's hearts to protect those you love. I get it." He then ran the 25 slants. He took the hit from Jeff. He lay on the ground as Jeff stood over him.

"If you ever, I mean ever, touch anybody or try to force yourself on any of God's kids, next time you will pay a much costlier penalty. Jesus said it would be better for a millstone to be tied around your neck and be thrown into the sea than cause one of God the Father's little ones to stumble. I will see you at Intervarsity on Tuesday night." Jeff left him lying on the ground and headed with the rest of the team back to the locker room.

Jack, despite his nose bleeding, could still smell the grass his was stretched out on. Every bone in his body hurt. Never had he been hit so hard and so many times. He lay flat on his back looking up at the blue Indiana sky. He could almost see the face of God in the puffy clouds over head. He knew something had to change. He knew at that second that his time in school had to be more than football. He just had to find out what God the Father through His Son Jesus by His Holy Spirit wanted to do with him. Since Jack was Catholic, he decided to go to one of the priests on campus and ask him.

The next day between classes he saw Father Schmidt walking down the hall. He walked up to him and asked a question. "Father, how do I know what part of God's purpose I am supposed to do?"

The good father looked at Jack and replied, "Jack, when you were a child you were baptized. At that point your parents made a commitment to raise you in the faith. There comes a time when you must decide who you are going to follow. Either you are going to follow our Holy Father through His Son Jesus by His Holy Spirit, or you are going to follow the enemy. As Scripture tells us, choose this day who you will serve?"

Jack smiled as he responded. "I choose to follow Christ. I have made a mess trying to run my own life. I will follow Jesus and serve him for the rest of my life." At that second Jack had a peace come over him like nothing he had experienced before. He looked at the father and said. "I feel like a new person."

Father Schmidt led Jack in a prayer of commitment to Christ. The excitement on Jack's face at the end of his prayer and new-found commitment to the Christ was an amazing thing to see and gladdened the Father's heart. When he walked into practice that afternoon, everyone knew that there was something new and improved about him.

The grin on Father Schmidt's face lit up the hallway. "My son, you have just experienced what it means to be born again. We Catholics feel it is offered at baptism. It's when you receive Christ that the long gestation period ends. Some people never experience it. Yet some who are willing to take that step and fully commit themselves to Christ experience the fullness in life that God has for them."

For the next hour Jack went up and down the hall of Notre Dame shaking hands and telling everyone one. "I have been born again." He skipped, and he jumped, he ran, and he jumped. He smiled, he hugged people. After practice on Tuesday night, he was at Intervarsity sharing with everyone there what had really changed his life.

The Father looked over at Peter. "Did you see how I took an evil that someone tried to perpetrate on someone and had that person put into a position where he would have to stop what he was doing to look up at me? Jack's football practice was painful and harsh. His warning was clear. He knew that Jeff meant what he said. His example was keen. Herman is an example of what a true gentleman should look like. Intervarsity is going to give him a view of what it truly means to be a believer in me. And what did it take? It took driving him to his knees. Sometimes I have to do that to have a person stop them looking at themselves and start looking at me."

"Father, that football practice was pretty vicious. When I was walking the earth, I would have been knocked out of the game with hits like that. You have built resilience into Jack." Peter responded.

The Father chuckled a bit. "Remember I have designed people to have a role in my service. I have a huge one for Jack. He is going to be a huge protector of the young ladies. He is going to marry, and you will have to wait and see what else I do with him."

Pete gave a bit of a chuckle. "What else is new!?"

# The Road to the Championship and After

Jack was now part of the team again. His attitude had changed from thinking he was the greatest to one of being part of the team. The team could now use him, as he realized it was not all about him, but about the team and their success. Because of what Christ had done, he could now be an excellent player and great example to people all around South Bend of what a true athlete should look and act like.

"Pete, remember Jamaal? I did what it took to get his attention. I will do that with anyone. I speak to people in ways they can hear me. I would that all men would be saved, but the ones who break my heart are the ones who know me and turn their back. Jack won't."

Coach Johnson decided to put a new play in for Jack. Because of his speed, Jack could get open on a short route and then explode for a big gain. It was set up so Jack would start from his slot back position, go in motion from left to right, and then break down field in an instant. Besides his swiftness, he could also stop on a dime and leave the opposition looking for their jock strap. This little "juke move" scored points galore for the Fighting Irish. Jake and Herman teamed up for many a victory.

The clincher came when they played the University of Minnesota for the National Championship. The Minnesota coaching staff had been watching that play repeatedly looking for that one step that would give away his cut. They thought they had found it. The problem was that Coach Johnson had figured it out as well.

Coach Johnson set up Jack as a decoy and then dropped a pass off to Ed Goldsmith the tailback running wide open down the sideline. It was over in a blink of an eye. Goldsmith scored, and Notre Dame won the National Championship with Herman Mcbrien as their quarterback.

The end of his sophomore year as quarterback produced some of the same feeling of emptiness after the big victory in high school. The team walked into the locker room hootin' and hollerin' but then the mood turned solemn as some of the team members started asking themselves what difference it made. What impact on the world could a game of football make?

Coach Johnson stepped in front of the team. "Men, I know there are huge emotions going through you right now. You worked hard all season. You won victory after victory.

You overcame adversity. Yet something is missing for some of you. On Monday you will go back to class. Everything will be the same as before the game. Nothing new. So why this game? Why is it so important? Each of you will have to ask yourself what you can do with this. What lessons have you learned?

The Father looked at Peter. "Pete, these young men are leaning a lesson that has been a tough one for young men since the beginning of time. These young men will have this victory in the back of their minds for the rest of their lives. The hard work to achieve it will serve them well all throughout their lives. Yet in the big scheme of things, it does not mean much. Nothing changes in the world. Their victory does not free anyone. It does not make a difference in the lives of the people who watched them play all season. Their names will be forgotten. But watch how Herman uses this."

Herman had, of course, been in this position before. He walked to the front of the room and looked at his teammates. "Gentlemen, I want to share with you something my father taught me. Victory is sweet for a short time, yet the platform it provides goes on much longer. We must use this platform that the Father in heaven has provided us to reach the people. We have just won a championship for one of the greatest institutions of higher learning in the world. Notre Dame means Our Lady. This is referring to the Mother of Jesus himself, Mary. We are to honor her Son Jesus in all that we do. We are to use this platform not to bring glory to ourselves, but to bring glory to the Most high God. She became a servant of the Highest. She called herself a handmaiden of the Lord when she spoke to Gabriel.

My brothers, some of us are going to be playing pro ball. Some of us are going to be powerhouses in business. Some of us are going to be educators on many different levels. But wherever The Father through The Son by His Holy spirit places us remember this. We can do all things through Christ who gives us strength. If we can keep Christ in the center of everything we do, we are going to see great things happen."

With that he turned and walked back to his bench in front of his locker and sat down.

Ed looked at Herman and just said, "Wow, where did you get that, man?"

Herman chuckled a bit. "When you have grown up in the home of two parents who are sold out to Christ, and when you have seen Christ work in your own life, it becomes just a bit natural. All one has to do is look around and see God's greatness in everything. I have two years left here, I hope we can win a couple more of these. This season was amazing. God has a purpose, and a role for each one of us in it. We just have to find that role."

"Pete, it's going to be fun guiding this kid for years to come. His mom and dad accomplished the role in getting him ready for what I have for him. He has proved to be totally sold out to me and my kingdom. Just watch what I do with him over the next couple of years."

The next morning Herman woke to the quiet of his on campus deluxe apartment. All was calm. He walked to the picture window that overlooked the campus. He observed the cars driving on the street. He could see the people strolling down the sidewalks of the streets on the campus in South Bend, Indiana. He poured himself a cup of coffee, looked up at the ceiling, and asked the Father, "What's this all about? My dad worked hard to accomplish greatness in baseball. He used that greatness to touch a lot of people. He gave ten years of his life to see Jamaal come to know you, and then Jamaal got himself killed. He could have touched so many more people. What is it you have for me to do?"

He walked over to the phone and dialed his dad's number. His dad answered on the other end.

"Hey, Champ, what's going on? Is everything alright?" Eli asked.

"Dad tell me this. I have been walking around my apartment all morning trying to make sense of this whole thing. We win a huge national championship. We accomplish some great things in football. For what? Why? How can this greatness accomplish anything long term? I just don't get it."

Eli got a concerned look on his face. "Herm, it's like this. Any sport in and of itself becomes a platform. God our Father through His Son by His Holy Spirit places each of us where he can use us to the maximum efficiency for his kingdom. Some folks are doctors, some are teachers, some are in businessmen and women, some work in a factory. Are we doing whatever we are created to do to the maximum of our ability? Are we holding nothing back? Are we optimizing our gifts so that we will see change in other people because of our gifts?"

Herman got a look of understanding on his face. "So, Dad, what you're telling me is that if I make the pros, I am there for one reason. That reason is to bring glory to the Father?"

Eli thought to himself, *"I would love to put my hand on his shoulder right now."* "No, son, that's not what I am telling you. If you get drafted when your college career is over, or if you don't, you are placed in critical positions in life where only you can touch people that our Father brings you in contact with. For instance, remember Lu from your high school years? God the Father is using her to touch a great many people at Gustavus. He is preparing her for a life of ministry in nursing. We are used wherever our Father puts us. What we have to remember that we have to be the best at where he places us. It's only then that we can accomplish the greatness he has for us."

"Dad, what I hear you saying is whether I am in class or on the field or in business after I graduate, I have to go at it 100%. If I am a dad or a priest, I go at it 100%. I don't hesitate to be the best at what I am doing. If I am in the workplace, I am a witness for Christ. If I am a parent, I do it as onto the Lord. As I do this it will open doors to touch people with the Gospel of Jesus Christ."

Eli smiled to himself. "Herman, you've got it. My son keeps that attitude and you will experience our Father's greatness in whatever you do. Don't ever back down from that which is right. God our Father through His Son by His Holy Spirit will keep you in the palm of His Hand."

"Pete, he's got it, he really does. Herman will have a huge impact on campus the next two years. More and more kids will come to know me through what I am doing with him. All he has to do is keep his eyes on me, and I will continue to accomplish greatness through him."

"Father will Herman make it to the pro level, and if so what team?" Peter asked with a sly grin.

"Pete, how many centuries have you been with me? You know I don't give away that kind of information. I invented classified information. But believe me, he will enjoy the ride as long as he keeps his eyes on me!"

Herman and his dad said their goodbyes. Herman walked across his room to once again look out the window. "*We have won a championship. I just feel that this championship is not what it is really about. I can't quite put my finger on it, but it's like the real reward is something else. It's like Paul said in I Corinthians 9. We must run the race. We must keep the prize in front of us. The prize is Christ and him crucified. The prize is the kingdom. All of this excitement over a football game is just that. Excitement over a game that has no consequences for anything. If we win there is excitement for a day. If we lose there is disappointment for a day. Life goes on. When a person come to know the living Christ, that excitement goes on forever.*"

He turned and walked away from the window. He walked to the door, deciding to go out for a walk. He opened it and to his great astonishment, Lucretia was standing there with her hand up ready to knock on the door. "Lu, what are you doing here?"

"My debate team is here in town. I thought it would be great to have coffee with an old friend. Probably best if we find a coffee shop rather than your apartment though." Lu said.

As they walked into the coffee shop on campus many students started to crowd around his table, eager to congratulate him on the big win. "Hey, guys, I am here with an old friend from high school. How about a little privacy so we can enjoy our coffee and conversation?" With that, the students left them alone.

"How in the world can you control a situation so easily?" Lu asked quizzically.

Herman smiled. "It's a matter of working both ways. During the season when someone, or many someone's for that matter, want some of my time I give it to them. So, when I tell them I really need privacy I get it. It's a give and take thing."

Lu smiled. "Cool."

The next two hours passed by quickly. As quickly as Lu came back into his life, however, she was soon gone again.

Over the next few days, Herman found himself thinking of Lu and wondering what might have been, until one morning while he was doing his devotional. "He who puts his hand to the plow and looks back is not fit for the kingdom." he read. "*Man, that puts everything into perspective. What is, is. We cannot go back. We should not be asking ourselves "what if?"* He closed his Bible and walked to the door, opened it, and went into the Indiana sunshine.

On that brisk day in January, he found himself wandering the streets of South Bend for hours. He walked by several churches wondering what doctrines they held on several topics.

The Father looked at Peter as he began to speak. "Pete, it's like this. Herman is at a turning point in his life. He still has strong feelings for Lucretia, yet he feels my call. All he has to do is say the word and the relationship between Lu and himself would be red hot. But he is seeking my face on where the rest of his life should go. The answer will not come this day, just more questions will come to mind."

Pete looked at the Father with a questioning look. "Father, your word says that all one has to do is ask and you give wisdom abundantly. Your word says seek and we will find. If a man seeks your word and the answer does not come, aren't you going back on your word?"

The Father of all mankind smiled as he said, "Pete, the answer always comes. The problem with mankind is he is not patient. The answer comes when it is needed. Remember this. When the time is right things happen. Herman will get all his questions answered. In my time."

All winter long, Herman worked out in the fieldhouse with the rest of his teammates. He was building his endurance as well as work on perfecting his passes. He looked forward to baseball in the spring. This would give him the break he needed. His passion for football was matched only by his love of baseball. His mind went back to the tales his dad would tell of the great games he had been in. His mind went back to Eli's tale of staring down the great Todd Rucket. His mind went back to the sharing of the game as he watched Jamaal Johnson in one of the few pro games he played before his life was cut short. It was at that second that Abby popped his bubble.

"Hey, Champ, don't forget we have that philosophy test to get ready for. And you are supposed to be working on disproving that atheist point that creation could not happen, remember."

Herman forced himself back to the present reality. He knew he had a bunch of research to do. Doc Thomas was a hard-nosed instructor who would not put up with a student trying to sneak by because of his athlete status. He knew he had to have a well-reasoned, well-researched, and factually supported paper to satisfy his professor.

The Father looked over at Peter. "He has trained both physically and intellectually for the job I have for him after his sports career is over. Herman is going to experience victories on the field and in the classroom. The biggest victories will come after he finishes his career on the field. I have lives for him to touch, and the platform he is building now in sports will serve him well. There are kids that I have planned to be born twenty years from now who are going to look up to him. Watch what I accomplish with him."

"Let me guess, no hints as to what you are going to do with this young man over the next forty years." Peter said smiling."

"Finally, Pete, you got it!" The Father responded.

It was Saturday morning. Herman was up early, in the gym working out. He was working with batters who were getting ready for the spring baseball season. He looked across the gym and saw Janet looking at him with her big brown eyes. She winked, and Herman started to flush.

"C'mon Mcbrien get your head back into the game. We have a brutal season coming at us and we need the greatest pitcher this team has ever seen pitching to us in a way that will make us be able to hit anyone." Johnson the outfielder hollered at him.

He used his dad's trademark move. He flipped the ball up over his shoulder into his glove and smiled at Johnson. The ball hit the catcher's glove at 95mph. Johnson was not even close.

"How's that?" Herman said with a grin.

Johnson was totally embarrassed. "All right, you proved your point. You are a great pitcher. Now make us great batters." Johnson replied.

Herman looked at Johnson. "My dad told me that any batter who is worth his salt will get video of the pitchers he is facing. Most pitchers are predictable. Not my dad. He knew what the batters were doing. He also had the Holy Spirit guiding him and getting little messages to him."

Thumbnail piped in as he spoke into Herman's ear. "I am the messenger that the Holy Spirit sent. Just me!"

Herman looked around himself and smiled. He knew what was going on. "Kyle Johnson, if you study hard, the Holy Spirit will bring to mind everything a pitcher is trying to do in any given game. I can throw fastballs that you can learn to hit. I can use all my different pitches, and you can learn to hit them, but sometimes you can translate that to another pitcher sometimes you can't. Watch the videos of the pitchers. Watch their stance. Watch their eyes. Then as you do all the above, pray."

Johnson nodded with full understanding what Herman was saying. "I think I get it. We have USC. next week. I better get studying these pitchers." He headed back to his dorm.

As Herman was walking out of the gym after practice, Janet walked up to him and put her arm through his. "Herman Mcbrien perhaps, just perhaps, it's about time that I took you aside and taught you there is more to life on this campus than being a sports hero." she said with a smirk.

Herman pulled his arm away from hers. "I suppose you could, but I won't. Look, Janet, there is a Fellowship of Christian Athlete's get together tonight. Why don't you join me?"

Janet got a look on her face that told him exactly what she thought of the idea. It was not good. "How can you blow me off that way? You holy rollers are all the same. You want to convert the world." Her voice held a note of pure disgust.

Herman chuckled to himself. "I am not out to convert the world. I am not even here to convert you. I just thought you might just enjoy a night out that is different than what you normally do."

Janet shook her head and stormed off. She could not seem to get it through her head just what purity was all about. She had never met a guy who did not want to just have a bit of fun, but Herman knew what was right and what was wrong.

The Father of all mankind looked over at His Son Jesus. "Son, Herman has the heart of a lion, and the gentleness of a dove." He then turned to Peter. "My servant Herman is not going to allow himself to be pulled into a situation that could destroy all that I have set my mind to do. He knew that by compromising a little bit he could hurt a lot of people. Just watch what I am about to accomplish through this young man. Thumbnail now is the time to try to get him excited about baseball. The sport is not as fast as football. But can be even more competitive between the pitchers and the batters. All though his life, Herman has led his teams to victory and championships just by his natural talent. He pitched because his team needed him, not because of his passion for the game. His passion is to walk up behind a center and look over the field and go with the called play or audible. On every play of every game it takes all eleven players on the field to make a play work. In baseball it's rare that you will see all nine players involved with a single play. And never will you see all the players involved with every play of every game.' '

The next day was game day. Herman walked out onto the baseball stadium at Notre Dame. There were a few students and people there ready to watch the game. What he did not notice was a pro scout from Los Angeles sitting in the stands. He heard Thumbnail speak into his ears.

"Herm, the Father knows your passion is football. He also knows that you learn a lot of kingdom truths playing football. But he wants you to know that just as in football if one player drops the ball the play fails, so to in baseball one player not doing his part hurts the whole team. Our Father in heaven created mankind to work together. Don't hold back but work extra hard for each victory."

Herman looked around himself trying to figure out just who was talking. He knew in his heart that what he was hearing was correct. He now understood that it does not matter the game, or for that matter anything people seek to endeavor to do in life. Teamwork is what will get it accomplished. It was at this point he knew just what was required of him for the rest of his college years. He would strive for high grades. He would be an excellent student. On the field whether baseball or football, he would accomplish as much as he could. He also knew, given the choice, he would play pro football rather than baseball, but he would play wherever the Father placed him.

The next two years flew by quickly. Herman achieved mastery in both football and baseball. His passion was still football. Los Angeles offered him a contract to play baseball, but the crowning achievement was being drafted by Minnesota to play football. On draft day Eli and Jill were sitting with him when Minnesota drafted him in the first round. The smile on his face lit up the room. He had taken the gifts that his Father in heaven had given him and used them to accomplish great things.

He knew that one thing was more important than anything else. He had to be about his Father's business. He just had to figure out how his Father in heaven wanted him to do that.

"Pete, Herman is now in a position where I can really use him. He has achieved greatness at his college level in both academics and on the playing field. This is going to be fun. When a person seeks me with their whole heart I can use them to accomplish great things in their lives and the lives of others. Now the fun starts."

"Father, am I correct in assuming you won't even give me a hint as to what you are going to do with him?"

With a chuckle, the Father looked at Peter. "You know me. I give information on a need to know basis. When you need to know I will tell you."

# Rookie of the Year or The Pain of it All

His senior year behind him, and two degrees, one in youth ministry and the other in communications, Herman was about to venture out into the world of professional football. Drafted in the first round by Minnesota, he was more than willing to walk away from baseball. "Father I know you have something you want me to do. Do I accomplish what you created me for by playing football, or is it after the game that things will get really interesting?"

The Father smiled as he looked over at Peter. "Pete, I think what Herman does not understand is that I have been using him at all stages of his life. From that first swim out to the raft, to his last snap as a college quarterback I have been using him as an example of what my servants really look like. Now I am moving him up to the pro ranks. He is about to find out what being tough is all about. It's not an easy thing to accomplish. But remember this. My word states that all things are possible for those who have placed their faith in Christ my Son."

Herman walked down from his room at the Hotel they were staying at. He saw Jill and Eli sitting at the table drinking coffee and reading the paper. They looked up at Herman as he walked in. "Morning Champ! Just reading your first newspaper article. Do not let this go to your head. Remember this. Our Father in heaven has work for you to do. That's why he has everything set up. You must make things happen but remember who is really in control. Kids' lives depend on it." Jill said.

*Minneapolis Star Gazette*

"Minnesota Picks Hometown Boy in First Round.".

He's the son of the greatest pitcher to ever step on the mound, Minnesota has picked Herman Mcbrien to be its quarterback of the future. Herm, also known as Mac, is quick on his feet and can throw a perfect spiral 75 yards and hit a dime. Coach Dennis Wolf, his old high school teammate has a lot of work ahead of him. Mcbrien played college football at Notre Dame after an all-star high school career with the Carlton, Minnesota Bulldogs. He will present no moral problems as a role model for kids as this young man. He practices what he preaches in everything he does. Minnesota's single females will be swooning. And he is smart too, graduating with a double major and a 3.9 GPA. Minnesota got a diamond in the rough with this young man.

The next morning Herman was having coffee with his mom and dad.

"Mom, Dad, where is this going to take me? I may be looking at ten or fifteen years of football here. Kids who are excited about me know, will be in their 30s when I retire. Shoot, I will be in my 30s or 40s when I retire. How does this work?"

Eli smiled. "Our Father in heaven has a plan. He sent his Son Jesus so that everyone could be saved. He used my career, and he will us yours as well. Your position with Minnesota is going to be a platform as much as mine was playing baseball. Just remember that you have one goal: to glorify our Father through His Son by His Spirit in all that you do. Don't quit, and you will see some great victories. Just keep your eye on the prize."

"I just wish Jamaal was here to see this." Herman got up and walked away knowing that he felt like crying. He had to get himself composed to be able to continue with that which his Father in heaven had called him to do.

Rookie Season.

August 2, 2030, Herman Mcbrien walked into the locker room for Minnesota. He looked around at some of the best football players in the country. The 6'5" John McDougal walked up to Herman. "Mcbrien, relax, you are about to take part in some of the hardest workouts you have ever taken part in. When they finish with you, you will be in the best shape you have ever been in. But don't forget your health depends on your line. Your longevity in this league depends on those of us who are going to protect you from those guys on the other side whose only intent is to crush you. We are here to make sure that does not happen. All we ask is when we take hard knocks to protect you is that you deliver the ball to our receivers, so we can score. All our paychecks depend on us winning. We all have base contracts. The big money is in the bonuses. The more we win, the more we make. I have seen your tapes. You're one of the best I have seen. Kids will look up to you. You will have a platform. Use it."

Thumbnail became excited. "Father, I got your message to John. Was it everything you wanted?"

The Father looked at his little angel. "You did well. You did really well."

Dennis Wolf, the new coach for Minnesota, walked into the locker room. "Gentlemen, we are about to embark on a path that will ultimately lead us to that championship that has eluded this team forever. This team has gotten close, but close is not good enough. We have worked hard to put together a team that is made up of men who are great both on and off the field. This team is made up of men kids can look up to. Parents will be able to point to people in every position and tell their kids that you are worth emulating. I am going to drive you to be the best you can be. I am going to drive you to overcome yourself. You will get to the point of quitting, but you won't. We will win." He turned and walked out.

The Father of all mankind looked over at Peter. "That's a lesson my church needs to hear every day. Sometimes people get so tired of the enemy throwing things at them they want to quit. It's the ones who refuse to quit who win. Remember my servant Joseph? He wanted to quit but did not. Or maybe my servant Jonah. He wanted to quit, but I would not let him. He won. Moses wanted to quit. He did not. He won. Herman is going to see times when he wants to just walk off the field. He won't. He will not quit. He will win."

Coach Wolf looked to Johnson one of his many assistants. He smiled and nodded. Johnson pulled out his bullhorn and ordered all seventy-five players to the goal line. "Gentlemen,

I am sure those of you who played basketball in high school remember the laker. That drill is where you run to the free throw line, then to mid-court, then the other free throw line, then to the boundary line on the other end of the gym. Gentlemen, you are getting ready for the last two minutes of the game. You will not run out of gas during a game if you are in the best shape you can be in. We intend to get you there. You will be paid a lot of money if you make this team. Veterans don't feel too good about your position. You are not safe. You will sprint to the 25, then to the 50, then to the 25, then to the other goal line. You will do these 10 times. On the line. Go!"

The first time through Herman was cruising. By the tenth he was hurting. His legs, his lungs, even his neck from the weight of his helmet. Every muscle in his 6'2" frame hurt. When he finished the set he crossed the goal line and threw up. Coach Wolf walked up to him, tapped him on the shoulder, and stood there and smiled. "Think you're good enough?" He asked as he looked Herman in the eyes with his cold stare.

"You know something, Coach. St. Paul wrote, 'I can do all things through Christ who gives me strength.' I have worked hard from the time I was a little kid. My teams have won a lot of championships. You can't break me. I will earn this position, Christ will be glorified by my play, and kids will have a player they can look up to." He turned and walked away thinking to himself. "*Hope I did not blow it there.*"

Coach Wolf smiled to himself as he muttered under his breath. "This will be great. This is gonna be fun."

The rest of training camp was tough, but Herman could see from the plays that Coach Wolf had put together that they had a real opportunity to accomplish some great things on the field, which would lead to great things off the field.

The month-long training camp finally came to an end. The new plays were going to be amazing to run, and Herman could not wait to see just how well they would work against the greatest football teams in the world. Six days of hard workouts had taken their toll. Herman was in the best shape of his life, yet his time with the Lord had been cut short by the time he had to spend in preparation for the season.

Coach Wolf had made sure that the team members who wanted to worship on Sunday had ample opportunity to do so. He also took part in the worship service. Wolf had brought in some great worship bands to lead their worship. Herman was astounded, however, at how badly some of his teammates were at singing. He could hardly keep from chuckling sometimes, but he realized in a new way what making a joyful noise really meant. As he watched some of his teammates really get into the worship experience, he began to see that the faith of Minnesota's football team was a unique thing.

Their first game of the season was against Los Angeles. Herman was on the bench for the first time ever. Greg Jones the fifteen-year pro led Minnesota to a 20-point victory over L.A.

After the game the team loaded onto the bus. Herman was almost the last one on the bus, and as he stepped up onto it, Coach Wolf looked at him and said, "Mcbrien, have a seat. We need to talk." Herman sat in the seat next to Coach Wolf. "Herman, you have a long career ahead of you. This is Jonesy's last year. This is his shot at a championship that may come along once in a man's lifetime. You can learn a lot from him. Be patient. When the time is right things happen. I mean, when the time is right, great things will happen. I am going to need every bit of talent that you have. This year is going to be a learning year for you. God has placed you on this team. Oh sure, the team went to a lot of trouble and time to scout you out. But God the Father through his Son by his Holy Spirit placed you here."

Herman looked at his coach. "I hear you, Coach. I was sent here to serve and to lead. I know that in order for me to do that effectually I have a lot to learn. I agree. When the time is right, things happen."

For the rest of the year Herman spent a lot of time with Jones. They talked defenses and attack strategies. They talked about passing to a point and looking for a receiver breaking free when he would be force to scramble. His rookie year was a year of gaining knowledge about what would be needed to see great things happen for the team. He got no press coverage; he did not see people swooning over him, but it was a great year.

# Season 2: Herman's Greatness Begins to Shine

HERMAN WAS READY FOR HIS training camp for the second year his pro football career. He had spent the off-season working out, forcing himself to be stronger and stronger. He had been in the weight room every day, building his arm strength. He knew he needed to be able to throw a football 60 yards and hit a dime. When he hit the practice field the first day, and they had the opening drill on the field he was able to run the 10 reps of the field more easily than he had the year before. He knew the last two minutes of many games would be key. He also knew that he had to be in shape to accomplish it.

The Father looked over at Peter. "Pete, he is learning that for my church to be great they have to be ready for the last "two minutes." Every member of my body has to work with the others to see more and more people brought to me. I arrange for people to meet. I will send a person miles to meet a person that I can use bring another person to me.

I start getting my servants ready when they are still in the crib. I know when a person is young whether they are going to serve me or not. Herman is serving me. I will use him in way that will surprise many people. I used him at Elim; I used him at Carlton High School I used him in college; I will use him here and beyond. But the key factor is he is willing to work. He is willing to put himself on the line daily and become what I have created him to be. He will be a superstar that kids will look up to and listen to. I give people platforms to work from. I use those people to accomplish great things, both in their careers and off the playing field. Watch Herman, Peter, this is going to be fun."

Herman woke Sunday morning. He had gone to mass the night before as he knew he needed to be in worship and he wouldn't be able to attend today. He knew they would be playing the team that had stopped them from getting into the playoffs last year.

He arrived at the stadium before most of his teammates. Bruce Johnson and Fritz Parker were there to meet him, so they could pray together before the game. To their surprise, Rod Davis and Lute Mullinex were there too, having heard about the prayer time before the game. Bruce and Fritz were linemen, Rod was a wide receiver, and Lute was one of the equipment managers. They spent an hour praying for each other's families as well of safety of all players on the field. They prayed that they would execute each play successfully and bring honor to the Father through the Christ by the Spirit in each situation they found themselves in. They all understood that football was a microcosm of life. Football plays could mirror life. They all knew that each game had its ebb and flows. They all knew that Coach Wolf had planned this game to a T. They knew that to beat the Wisconsin Butchers, they would have to employ every aspect of their game. They knew it would be a tough game, and if they wanted the ultimate victory that season, they had to get past this spot to achieve it.

The National Anthem was played. They won the toss and elected to give the ball to the Butchers first. The Butchers quarterback called a quick pass over the middle, hoping to loosen up the defense. It did not work. The ball was tipped by Parker, grabbed by Johnson, and returned for a touchdown. Herman went on to throw two touchdown passes and lead his team to a 21-14 victory. After the game, to locker room was total bedlam. Herman stood up on a bench to yell over the din. "Gentlemen, do you mind if we have a prayer? I think it's appropriate that we do so." The locker room went silent. Herman led in a prayer of thanksgiving. As soon as the prayer was over, the locker room once again became a place of noisy celebration.

Over the next fifteen weeks, the team would finish the season with a record or 12 wins and 4 losses, which was good enough to win their division and make the playoffs. They had a bye the first week. Herman was able to go home and visit his mom and dad. As he arrived at the house, his parents flew at him with hugs of excitement. "Son, we are so proud of you. You have led the team on the field and off is amazing. The world can see God the Father through His Son by His Holy Spirit working through you." Eli then gave him another bear hug.

His younger sister ran down the stairs. "Hermy, I have missed you so much. How are you?" she yelled with total excitement.

Herman turned and gave his sister hug. "Sis, I am doing great. The Lord has been really good to me.

"Lu has been asking for you." she said offhandedly.

"Don't know I will have time to see her. I am only home for a couple of days, and then I have to get back for practice on Tuesday." he said with a note of sadness in his voice.

The next couple of days passed quickly. He went to church at Elim with his parents on Sunday after a Saturday mass in Carlton. Both Saturday night and Sunday morning Holy Communion was celebrated. As he walked out of Elim Sunday morning, Lu was waiting at the bottom of the steps. "How ya doing, Champ?" she greeted him warmly.

He ran down the steps stopping at the bottom to give Lu a big hug. "I am great, the playoffs should be interesting. I have never played at this level. Win or lose, God the Father will be glorified. He knew this was not a time to get involved with anyone. He had to stay focused on the game at hand.

His mom and dad walked out of the church. They saw him talking to Lu. She nodded and turned and walked to her car, got in, and drove away. The walked over to Herman and asked him what was going on.

The Father looked over at Pete. "Pete, sometimes tough choices have to be made. I have had my spirit speaking to Herman's heart for a long time. Herman is set apart. He has to be focused on me and my kingdom. There is a time and a season for all things. This is not the time or the season for him getting involved with any one. This is the time in his life when he has to dedicate himself to me. Just watch and see what I do with this young man."

"Dad, it's like this. For whatever reason it seems like God our Father does not want me involved with anyone. I heard this little voice tell me that I have been set apart for the kingdom. I am not sure what that means at this point in my life. I really would have loved to have gone to lunch with Lu today. I just could not. It's like I could not give her anything because I really feel that she would have wanted more, and

I could not have given it to her. I remember when we had our last motorcycle ride together. Something happened, I realized at that time that I could fall in love with her, but it was like I was being stopped from going any farther. I had to say goodbye. I got on the bike and never looked back." He threw his arms around his dad and cried. "Dad, I wanted to turn around and go back, I just couldn't."

Eli looked at Jill. She had a tear running down her cheek. "Let's talk later." she said holding back the sobs.

When they arrived home Jill and Eli went down a trail in the woods walking hand in hand. "Eli how could a loving God tell Herman not to be interested in a great Christian girl who is still hopelessly in love with Herman?"

Eli stopped on the trail, turned and looked Jill right in the eyes. "Hun, it's like this. What we see is in front of our faces. God the Father through His Son by His Holy Spirit sees way beyond what we can see. It's like Joseph in Egypt. When his brothers threw him into the pit, he had no idea that it was going to land him in Pharaoh's court being second in command to Pharaoh himself. Our Father in heaven has something special in mind for Herman. Getting involved would probably put a quick stop to that plan. That's why he is not to be involved with anyone. One other thing. We don't know that Father has someone else in mind for both."

Jill smiled, threw her arms around Eli and simply said. "Hun you're so tuned in with what the Father is doing. I really do love you." Eli smiled.

That night Herman drove back to the Twin Cities. He had to get ready to play the Branson Bulls in the playoffs. The week was a grind. Branson was a tough team. Their record showed it as well. Their coach, Tom Hughes, never stopped pushing his players. They did not mind because they won a lot of games playing this way. Herman knew this game would be different than most. He knew their pass defense was brutal. Hughes had trained his players to show no mercy when they hit a receiver. He understood that a lot of passes were dropped because of the brutal hits the opposing receivers took. The most important thing going through his mind was to make sure he put the ball in close to his receivers to protect them from "lay-out" hits.

The game was tough. It would be all out war on the field. The hits from both teams were nothing short of brutal. In the end Minnesota would lose. Next year was coming!"

"Pete, when I put it in Walter Camp's mind to invent football, I had many reasons for doing it. First and foremost, I did it to show the players life lessons. As I look at Herman, I see a young man who has learned these lessons well. Winning the game is the purpose. Keeping his players as safe as possible is essential to that victory.

It's the same with my servants. Winning my children's souls is important. But I will protect those I have created who do the work. My kingdom is built on teamwork. My players can learn some very valuable lessons from this game."

This season was tough. As a second-year player, and his first year starting, Herman found himself making some not so smart choices, but Coach Wolf never gave up on him. The team finished 10 and 6, making the playoffs in a wild card position. This year's playoff run was short lived. They were defeated quickly.

Season 3

Herman looked up. In walked a huge player, a 6'6 fullback, blonde hair shining as he walked into the dressing room. "Who are you?" Herman asked.

"Tommy Johnson, I was brought over in a trade from Dallas. And who are you? "He answered.

"I'm Herman Mcbrien. They call me the quarterback around here."

"Any relations to Jill Mcbrien? Tommy asked.

"Yup, that'd be my mom. Do you know her?"

"Not well. I only met her in a restaurant many years ago. She saved my life!" Tommy replied.

Herman got a real quizzical look on his face. "How?" he asked.

"Your mom and dad were having breakfast in probably the nicest restaurant in town. My mom and I had a window seat overlooking the Pacific Ocean. I saw your dad. He had just recently played his last game. He had just won the seventh game of the World Series. I asked mom for the little notebook she had in her purse. I walked over to the table and asked your dad for an autograph. I asked him to sign it for my mom because I would not be around much longer. Herman, your dad was and is a great man. He went over and talked to my mom and asked her some questions. The next thing I knew, your mom was donating some of her bone marrow to me. I think I am eight or nine years older than you. I have a couple of good years left in me. When word circulated that Minnesota was looking for a good back to help you, I went to the front office and asked for a trade. Don't get me wrong. I loved playing for Dallas. It was my dream team. But I had to play with you. I felt a compulsion that would not quit. I had to get here. I explained the whole situation to the front office. And they went along with it. It seems they did a lot for me. I had better produce and really help this team."

A stunned Herman picked up his cell. "Hi, mom! Can you and dad drive down tomorrow? I would love to take you guys out to dinner. Where? How about Dave's in Forest lake. That way you guys aren't driving as far, and we can meet you there. No mom the we is not me and a young lady for you to meet. But you will be surprised."

The next night Herman picked up Tommy in his Corvette. As they cruised into Dave's parking lot, they got out of the car and walked into the best rib place in the Twin Cities. As he walked in, there was a young boy sitting with his mom and dad. He looked like he might be hyperventilating. Herman smiled at Tommy and said, "Let's go over there."

They walked over to where the family was sitting. "Hi, I am Herman Mcbrien, and this is our newest running back, Tommy Johnson."

The young boy was so excited he was bouncing in his seat. His smile was a mile wide. "Could I get your autographs?"

Tommy looked at the young lad and saw that his white t-shirt had the Minnesota logo on it. "I bet we could sign your t-shirt." Tommy said.

Herman chuckled. "How about we sign the t-shirt, and we also have a couple of team caps in the car we could sign as well."

Herman walked out to his Vette, grabbed a couple the caps from the trunk and came back in. "I have three of them. Mom, Dad, and..."

"Johnny." the young lad stated emphatically.

Herman looked up to see his mom and dad sitting in a corner where the hadn't noticed them earlier. "Mom, Dad, how long have you been here?"

"Oh, about fifteen minutes. Long enough to be bursting our buttons with pride. You made that kid's day." Eli said.

Tommy walked over to Jill and Herman. "He learned well from some great parents. I'm Tommy Johnson.".

"What do you mean?" Jill asked.

"Think back to when you met a young boy with Leukemia a bunch of years ago. You gave him some of your bone marrow. I am that little boy."

Jill's eyes started to water as she began to cry. "So, you're going to be playing for Minnesota this year?"

"Absolutely, I really felt like our Father in heaven wanted me here. Now I know why. I think we should work to build up the bone marrow bank. If it had not been for God our Father through His Son by His Holy Spirit having you in the restaurant that day, I would not be here. I am about two-thirds of the way done with my medical degree. I feel like the part of God's purpose I am going to take care of."

The Father looked over at Pete and said. "Pete, I started plans for this event 4000 years ago. There is a saying I have given to one of my servants who tends to get a bit impatient. When the time is right things happen. When the time was right they met in a restaurant, when the time is right they meet again in Minnesota. The first meeting of Herman and Tommy is going to lead to some great victories over the next few years. When people give me the credit they will see great victories. This is gonna be fun."

The two seemed to be like brothers. Both men understood one truth. They were both alive and playing for a professional football team in Minnesota because Jill Mcbrien had given them both life – one through birth, the other from a bone marrow transplant. They both understood what being born anew really meant because of this experience.

Training camp was challenging. The two men had worked out hard in the off season. They had prepared for this eventuality. They had decided in the off season that this training camp would be a time of learning the plays more effectually and not pooping out on the training field.

After a dismal pre-season the team got ready for the regular season. They had lost all four-pre-season games by large margins, but the team was ready for the regular season. Their first game would be against the Butchers of Wisconsin.

Coach Wolf introduced a new play to his team. "We will use it only once during the whole season. It will catch the defense we are going to playing against off balance."

Herman looked at Coach Wolf. "We used that in State Championship. Coach Erickson said after he used it, he used it only once. We know what play that was, and we know how effective it was." Herman had a big smile on his face.

"Gentlemen, we are going to practice this play every day. You will be able to do it in your sleep. Those few seconds it takes to do it will be heaven when it is successful. We will see glory from it. Then we will honor Jim Erickson after the game. It will be used when the game is on the line, and it is do or die. "

The Father looked at St. Peter. "Pete, what you are about to see is a whole season dedicate to one man who has earned honor in his players' eyes. I could tell when Jim was young that he would serve me. Now I am going to have him honored with a season that is going to end with a play that will blow people's minds. You see for him to use it in high school he had to have just the right players. In the pros it is much easier to pull this off as your talent set will be there. Just remember this. When the game is on the line, they are going with whom they can trust."

"Who is that?" Peter questioned the Father.

The Father just smiled.

As the regular season got underway the team gelled. Team after team that came against them went down. Sixteen weeks went by in a hurry. As the end of the season approached, Minnesota was the team to beat. They had one thing on their mind, bringing the trophy back to Minnesota.

The playoffs were tough. Even though they had home field advantage throughout the playoffs, it was very difficult to take out both Dallas and Los Angeles, but they did it. They made it to the NFA Championship. Ft. Worth was their opponent. Down by 2 and on the 50-yard line there was only one thing to do. Herman dropped back and hit Tommy for the winning touchdown with no time left. They were going to the big game. It would be super.

The Last Hurrah!

Tommy and Herman were having dinner. "Hermy, you do know I would not be here if it weren't for your mom, don't you?"

Herman got a quizzical look on his face. "What do you mean?"

"When I was 10 and had leukemia that would have been fatal if I had not had a bone marrow transplant. A "chance" meeting in a restaurant on the beach had me trying to get your dad's autograph for my mom. The rest is history. You mom turned out to be a match. We are playing football together for one season. I retire at the end of the next game."

Herman gave a bit of a chuckle. "Then we better win it, so you can go out a winner."

"Herm, there would be nothing that would bring me more joy than to give your mom my championship ring as a thank you." Tommy stated with a tear in his eye.

That week they went over play after play, but the one play, the play, was the one Coach Erickson put together years before when Herman played for Erickson in high school.

Herman walked up to Coach Wolf. "Do you really think a high school play will beat these guys?"

Wolf gave a chuckle. "Herm, watch, just watch. You do your job, and this will catch them completely off guard."

The game was a slugfest. With two seconds left Denver was leading by 4.

"Hello, this is Tim Johnson and Kyle Smotherwood with ABD Sports."

"Tim what do you think of Minnesota's quarterback? Herman Mcbrien has been having a great season this year. For a third-year player, his passing has been pin point on." Kyle stated with excitement.

"Kyle, we are sitting here with two seconds left on the clock. Minnesota is trailing by 4 points. A field goal does them no good whatsoever. Their coach Dennis Wolf has something up his sleeve. He has made calls all season long that have made his team shine. But what could he possibly have in mind now?"

"Tim, look over at the sidelines. There is something you don't see very often. Both Mcbrien and Tommy Johnson are huddled with the coach on the sidelines. They are cooking up something, but I don't have a clue what's going on. If you check out the skybox you will see Tommy's mom Janice and Eli and Jill Mcbrien talking about what could be up their sleeve as well. Do you have any clue what could possible in the works?"

Tim replied. "Kyle, they seem to be praying. I do know that both families have a deep faith in Christ and they depend on him for everything. But prayer for a football game? Sure, this is the Super Bowl, but prayer for a football game?"

Tommy looked intently at Coach Wolf. "Coach, what your calling here is the play. If it works you are a hero for having the guts for calling it. But..."

Coach Wolf looked intently into the faces of his two players as he said. "This play has to be something they have no clue is coming. They know every play in our book. The two of us have one thing in common. We both played our high school ball under Jim Erickson. Just at different times. We have everything against us here. When it comes to the last play who do you trust?"

Herman looked directly into Wolf's eyes. "I trust God our Father. And I know exactly what I am going to say when we get to the line." He said with an intensity in his voice that surprised even him.

Wolf looked at his men and only had one thing left to say. "Get 'er done!" Both men headed back to the huddle.

The two men reached the huddle. The clock would start running at the snap of the ball. Herman barked out the signals. "Power right, 26 crash sweeps left. Pass left 36 crosses 25 fly. On 2. Break!"

Both teams lined up on the ball. Eli bent down under center and started to bark out the signals. "35,22, Not by might, not by power, but by my spirit, says the Lord." The whole Cleveland team looked up. When they did Eli yelled "Go."

Tommy took a step back and ran behind Eli who flipped him the ball. Looking like he still had it he sprinted right like he was going to throw down to Bruce Johnson his fullback. Johnson cut sharply to the sideline. They had him covered tight as he had been giving them fits all day.

Herman cut up field then turned on the afterburners and got wide open and streaked for the end zone.

Tommy set and made a perfect throw. The ball soared through the January frost towards the end zone.

Twenty-one years earlier a 10-year-old sports nut named Tommy sat across from his mom in a cozy restaurant in southern California. Tommy looked over and saw his hero sitting there. The little boy knew just how sick he was and knew he would not be around much longer, and he wanted to give his mother to remember him by. He pointed Eli out to his mom, grabbed a piece of paper and headed for Eli and Jill's table.

The Father looked over at Peter. "I have something special in mind for the young lad. I arranged for everyone to be where they are today. "

Pete just looked at the Father knowing what the answer would be if he asked. "Just wait and see."

Tommy headed for Eli and Jill's table. He walked up and looked at Eli and Jill and could not say anything. He was dumbfounded. Eli spoke first.

The boy answered, in somewhat in a weak voice, "My name is Tommy. You see, I would like her to have something special to remember me by."

Eli looked at his mom, then at Jill. "Tommy, what's your mom's name?"

Tommy looked at his mom. "Janice."

Mr. McBrien, I am not going to be here much longer. Could you make it out to my mom?

Eli excused himself and walked to the other side of the restaurant where Janice was sitting. "Janice, what's wrong with Tommy?"

"Tommy has a rare form of leukemia. There is only one bone marrow transplant in a million that will work. He has O-negative blood."

Eli excused himself, walked over to his bride, and gave Jill a kiss on the cheek. "Hun, you have O-negative blood, don't you?" he asked.

Jill got a puzzled look on her face. "Yes, why?"

"Go talk to Tommy's mom for a moment," he asked ever so sweetly.

"Pete, do you see how in this instance, all things will work for the good, and does this help you understand divine appointments?" The Father continued, "This may help you understand why I do what I do."

Pete answered, "Yes, Father, I think I do."

Jill walked over to Janice, "What is wrong with Tommy?"

Janice had tears running down her cheek as she told Jill what the problem was.

Jill looked at Janice and started crying. "I had a miscarriage last month. We lost a little girl. Why don't I get checked? If my marrow is a match, then we can use it."

All Janice could say was, "Thank you!" Not holding much hope that it would work.

Before Jill and Eli were able to arrive back at their condo, Jill's phone rang. "This is Jill. Yes…aha…we'll be there. Two o'clock. That will be fine."

Eli, with a very questioning look on his face, asked, "What was that about?"

"I have an appointment to check my bone marrow, to see if I am a match for Tommy," was the sweet answer his beautiful bride gave. "

Herman looked up and saw the ball coming directly towards him. He held out his hand, and the ball dropped lightly into his arms like a loaf of bread. TOUCHDOWN! The crowd went wild.

That was Tommy's last play from scrimmage. He retired and went into medicine and worked in youth Ministry. Herman played for another ten years. He did not win another Super bowl, but he had a successful and well-regarded football career. After his last season, retired and joined the Catholic priesthood.

Three months after the Super bowl win, Tommy knocked on Eli and Jill's door. "Mrs. Mcbrien. I want you to have this. It's my Championship ring. Without what you did for me with the bone marrow I would not be here to win it. I want you to have this."

"Tommy, I hear you are going to be a youth minister. Just think of the stories you can tell all those kids about how important it is that they look at everyday as a gift. That they take their gifts and work hard with them to be the best they can be. I will take a hug. Nothing more. Just remember this. God our Father through His Son by His Holy Spirit gives us each gifts. We have an obligation to work as hard as we can to use those gifts to reach into other people's lives and see them come to the Christ."

Tommy smiled and hugged Jill. He turned and gave a huge bear hug to Eli as well. With tears running down his and sobs abounding, he turned, looked at his ring, said a heartfelt thank you, and walked to his car.

Herman played another 10 years and answered the call that was put on him from his youth. He went into the priesthood to head the youth dept of St. Johns University.

Writing the Eli series has been a joy in my life. I want to thank my Father in heaven by His Son through His Spirit for giving me these three books. Many of the names in this book are old friends and team mates. Thank you. Our lives are touched by many people. To all my readers be blessed.

Michael D. Goldsmith

12358823R00106

Made in the USA
Middletown, DE
22 November 2018